A Family's Code

by

Ursula Renée

The Santiano Family

A Family's Code

Cover Art by *Lisa Dawn MacDonald*

The Wild Rose Press, Inc.
PO Box 708
Adams Basin, NY 14410-0708
Visit us at www.thewildrosepress.com

Publishing History
First Edition, 2025
Trade Paperback ISBN 978-1-5092-6181-9
Digital ISBN 978-1-5092-6182-6

The Santiano Family
Published in the United States of America

Dedication

This is dedicated to my son, who has always encouraged my dreams.

Prologue

June 28, 1951

Matteo Santiano had always done what he was told. As a child, he followed his father's directions and headed straight home from school every afternoon. He never dawdled when his mother sent him to the store for eggs and milk. And his teachers never had to give him a demerit for incomplete assignments. Therefore, when told to do right by the woman he knocked up in the backseat of a convertible, he did not hesitate to give her his name…a decision he regretted since the day he said, "I do."

The squeal of the second-floor window dragging along the track shattered the peace Matteo had been relishing since storming out of the two-family brick house. He prayed Eleanor would be struck with a sudden bout of laryngitis. Yet, before he could bargain a year of perfect attendance at Sunday mass in exchange for another minute of silence, a high-pitched shrill filled the air.

Groaning, Matteo lifted his head from his hands and pushed away from the tan sedan he had been leaning against. He glared across the street at his wife, who leaned out of the window. Her red hair whipped around her like angry flames as she accused him of forcing her to live in poverty.

Two women strolling down the block shook their

heads, silently reprimanding him for the transgressions. Had it not been for the headache developed from his wife's complaints, Matteo would have laughed in their faces. In a neighborhood where the average salary was less than four thousand dollars a year, he believed the two-hundred-dollar allowance she received each month in addition to the five hundred he provided for the household expenses was more than generous.

Matteo slammed his palm on the hood of the car. "*Chuidi la bocca!*"

Instead of shutting her mouth, Eleanor accused him of stealing her emerald ring…a claim he had been denying since their wedding day, as he could not steal jewelry his grandmother refused to part with despite an earlier promise to pass it on to his wife.

The five minutes of pleasure he got under the stars in the empty parking lot had not been worth the lifetime sentence that followed. Yes, a beautiful daughter had been produced from the union, but with her came a shrew even Petruchio could not tame.

The cloudless sky and warm breeze did little to ease the throbbing in Matteo's temples. He needed something stronger, like a gag or a shot of whiskey. Figuring the latter would be easier to obtain, he climbed into the car and peeled down the street.

Matteo sped to Sugar, the Bedford Stuyvesant bar owned by an acquaintance of the family. He had no intention of patronizing the establishment that got most of its business from the coloreds who lived in the neighborhood. Instead, he would stick his head into the apartment over the business to inquire if the residents knew the whereabouts of his cousin Nicholas, whose sister was best friends with the daughter of the owner.

He arrived at the bar the same moment a delivery truck pulled away from the curb. Matteo slid into the parking spot, jumped out of the car, and ran up the steps to the residential portion of the building. The sunlight poured through the propped-open door into the foyer. The overwhelming odor of paint warned him against touching the beige banister as he headed up the freshly polished marble staircase.

On the second level, he knocked on the first door to his right before stepping into the apartment. The silence that greeted him confirmed the girls he was searching for were not around. Had they been at home, their snickers and squeals would have filled the space.

On the off chance James Collins was inside and not at the bar, Matteo called out, "Anyone home?"

A sniffle was the only reply.

Matteo pushed the door closed behind him and walked into the living room. The curtains were drawn against the afternoon light, yet the dim glow from the lamp on the end table and a soft mew helped him locate the girl sitting in the corner staring at the hands lying in her lap. Strands of hair escaped from the short ponytail that barely reached the collar of her brown uniform.

The teenager, who was no older than fifteen or sixteen, had attended his wedding reception. She had worn a loose-fitting dress that did not completely hide the bump that indicated his bride was not the only one in attendance in a family way. But with more than enough problems of his own to worry about, he had barely offered her a second glance before greeting the next person passing by the receiving line.

"Nick around?" he asked.

She took in a ragged breath, then replied, "He took

Georgia and Celeste to Coney Island."

Matteo muttered a curse. It would be several hours before Nicholas drove the girls home…and then it would still be a matter of which dwelling they would return to. The girls divided their time between each other's homes, and there was no telling where they would be until they settled in for the night.

The girl sniffled and wiped a tear from her brown cheek with her fingers. Though her head hung low, he suspected there were more tears preparing to fall.

Matteo glanced back at the door. He desperately wanted a drink, not the burden of someone else's problem. Yet while his mind ticked off the reasons he should walk away, his feet carried him to the corner.

"Hey, kid, what's wrong?" He crouched by her side and hooked a finger under her chin.

He lifted her face until he could see her trembling lip and the tears hovering at the rim of her brown eyes.

Between her thick, southern accent and her sob, he barely understood her whispered, "I'm scared."

Matteo's brow wrinkled. He saw no reason for her to be afraid.

The sun had yet to set. There were plenty of people milling about on the street who could hear her screams if someone bothered her. And there were no creatures, more afraid of her than she was of them, scurrying along baseboards.

"What's there to be afraid of…?" He paused when his gaze fell on the arms cradling her engorged stomach. "Ah, dammit." It was a good thing his mother talked him out of following in the footsteps of the Hardy Boys when he was ten. He would have made a poor detective. "When did the pains start?"

"This morning…" She hiccupped before adding, "After I got to work."

"Why didn't you tell your boss?"

She sniffled. "I did. She told me to finish cleaning the bathroom and then go home."

Matteo gripped the edge of her chair. He must have heard wrong. No woman was heartless enough to demand someone do housework while in labor.

The strong odor of pine on her hands and the water stains on her dress indicated the girl was not exaggerating.

"Where's your uncle?" He did not bother asking about the father of her baby. Her staying with her relatives said it all. Lover-boy had taken off when he was told she was with child.

The girl shook her head. "He said he was taking a loan payment to Mr. Santiano."

Matteo recalled the arrangement his uncle and Mr. Collins made for the latter to purchase the bar. On the last Thursday of each month, the men met to settle accounts and discuss the business. The meeting always ended with his uncle inviting the other man to lunch.

Unfortunately, aside from a telephone call to each establishment, there was no way of knowing which one of his uncle's favorite restaurants the men had decided to patronize and how long the meal would last. If Matteo's father and several other friends joined them, lunch could turn into dinner and then midnight drinks before they called it a night.

Matteo had never seen anyone look as miserable as this girl. Unlike his wife, who pitched a fit because he refused to give her money for a new bracelet, the girl had real problems. She was alone and, he was willing to bet a small fortune, she had no idea what to expect.

"Are the pains bad?" he asked.

"It feels like the pains I get with my monthly," she replied.

"How often do you feel them?"

"The last one was at two forty-five."

Matteo glanced at his watch. It was three fifteen. Thirty minutes apart wasn't bad. She had plenty of time.

He had driven Eleanor to the hospital when her contractions were every twenty minutes, only to be sent back home with instructions to return when the pains were ten minutes apart.

"There's nothing to be afraid of." He lowered his voice, hoping the softer tone would help ease her fears. "My wife gave birth last month. I'm an expert at this."

The corners of her lips pulled back.

"If you'd like, I'll drive you to the hospital, then look for your family."

"Y…you would?" The surprise in her voice did not come close to Matteo's shock.

Where the hell did that offer come from? She was his cousin's best friend's cousin, or—in layman's terms—a stranger he was under no obligation to help. A simple offer to carry her bag downstairs and hail a cab would have sufficed.

The girl's wide eyes glistened with hope. Her expression was much different from his wife's perpetual scowl, which would silently demand a reply that met with her approval.

The second hand on the clock ticked six times before Matteo nodded his head. It wouldn't kill him to put aside his petty troubles to help someone in need.

"Of course I would." He wiped the tears from her

cheeks with the back of his hand. "I just need one thing from you."

"What's that?" she whispered.

"Your name." He tilted his head and raised an eyebrow. "I can't check you into the hospital under Kid."

Her grin widened. "Bailey Collins."

"It's nice meeting you, Bailey Collins." He held out his hand. "I'm Matteo."

"I remember." She slipped her rough hand into his. "We were introduced at your reception."

Matteo felt like a jerk. Yes, he had a lot on his mind during his wedding, but even with the prospect of raising a child by herself, she had taken the time to remember his name.

Matteo took both of her hands in his and stood. "Go wash your face and get your things," he said, pulling her to her feet.

Bailey grabbed the clear tote sitting next to the chair and waddled towards the rear of the apartment. If his memory served him correctly, the apartment contained only one bedroom. With her uncle occupying the living room, it meant she had to share the small sleeping quarters with her cousin. The space would be even smaller when she returned from the hospital with the baby. They would not be able to turn around without bumping into each other.

Matteo pulled a flask from the inside pocket of his jacket. A nip of whiskey would have to do until he dropped Bailey off at the hospital and found someone who could take up the search for her family. Once free, he would find some place to enjoy a shot or maybe something stronger to help him temporarily forget his troubles.

7

"I'm ready." Bailey walked into the living room wearing a faded blue dress with a white collar. She had scrubbed her face and secured her hair in a French roll.

Matteo slipped the flask back into his pocket. "Where's your suitcase?" He mentally scolded himself for not offering to retrieve the bag. With the clothes and toiletries, she would need to get through the next couple of days, plus everything she packed for the baby, the luggage had to be too heavy for her to carry.

Bailey held up a brown paper shopping bag. "Here it is."

Matteo took the bag and peeped at the toothbrush lying on top of a green dress he had seen her cousin wear the previous year.

"That's it?" The question spilled from his mouth before he could stop himself.

Her shoulders slumped and her head dropped. "I can't afford a fancier dress, with a baby on the way."

He mumbled an expletive. Could he be any more of an ass? Hell, while he was at it, maybe he should give her a lecture about the evils of sleeping with someone before she recited vows.

Matteo had no right judging the girl. If he had not stepped up and married Eleanor, she could have found herself in the same situation. Therefore, if he was not going to be a part of the solution, he needed to walk away…something his conscience would not let him do.

"Come on." He tossed her scant belongings onto the chair and grasped her hand.

"Wait! What about my clothes?"

"We can do better than that," Matteo said, guiding her towards the door.

Bailey glanced back at the bag one more time before

following him. He led her out of the building and helped her into the car before climbing behind the wheel.

"The hospital's the other way," she noted when he made a right at the corner.

"We have a stop to make," he replied. "How are you feeling?"

She shrugged a shoulder, a gesture he interpreted to mean she was still scared but determined to put on a brave face. He reached across the seat and patted the hands folded in her lap.

The sparse traffic and his lead foot had Matteo pulling up in front of the Livingston Street entrance of A&S fifteen minutes later. He would have preferred to take her to the city, but he did not want to waste time making the trip and then searching for a salesclerk who would be willing to help Bailey despite the darker hue of her skin, the circumference of her stomach, and the lack of jewelry adorning the third finger of her left hand.

"You want to come in with me or wait out here?" Matteo asked as he switched off the engine.

"I'll come in," she replied, reaching for the door.

Matteo jumped out of the car and jogged around before her right foot touched the sidewalk. He took her hand and escorted her into the department store, ignoring the passersby who had nothing better to do than gawk.

They weaved around perfume and makeup counters on the main level to reach the bank of elevators. With no one else in the car, they were treated to express service to the eighth floor, where he figured they could start their excursion and work their way down.

"Pick one." Matteo waved at the suitcases and overnight bags of various material, sizes and colors as they strolled into the luggage department.

He assumed with such a vast selection it would take her a while to choose. Yet she headed straight for a powder-blue bag with a lace trim around the neck.

Matteo chuckled at her vain attempt to reach the bag sitting on the top shelf. Even standing on the toes of her flat, soft-soled shoes, her fingers were an inch shy from her selection.

Without exerting any more energy than it would take to scratch his brow, Matteo grabbed the bag.

"Show off," she mumbled when he passed the suitcase to her.

"No, you're short," he said.

"I'm no shorter than the average woman."

That would put her between five-foot-four and five-foot-six. He towered over her by at least six inches, which in his book meant she was, as he said, "Short."

"Whatever you say…Stretch."

She had a sense of humor, something Matteo had come to appreciate. With so much in the world that could get them down, people needed to find something they could smile about.

Feeling more relaxed than he had in months, he paid for the bag, then led her through the store, picking up everything he recalled his wife shoving into her suitcase weeks before she would head to the hospital. He watched for signs that Bailey's labor progressed, but other than grimacing twice, she showed no evidence of trouble.

"How you are holding up, Shorty?" Matteo asked when they arrived at the final register on the second floor.

She rolled her eyes. "You forgot my name again?"

"No, I didn't forget your name."

"Then what is it?"

"Bailey, smarty-pants."

"Wrong. It's Bailey Collins."

The joke had to have been the worst he had ever heard, yet she was no longer frowning and had ceased twiddling her fingers. He would rather have a relaxed woman than a comic on any day.

"That'll be twenty-four sixty-three," the cashier announced with a frosty tone. Her eyes narrowed as she glared at Bailey.

Matteo retrieved his wallet from his back pocket and produced a twenty and a ten. The woman bristled when she slid the money from his hand and revealed his extended finger.

Bailey covered his hand with hers. "You're being rude," she whispered.

He would have patted himself on the back for achieving his goal had her gaze not been darting around the room as if she expected trouble. Her nervousness reminded him of their differences. While he would not stand for someone to disrespect him, she had very little choice. Where she came from, speaking up could have dire consequences if one did not possess the proper pedigree.

He turned his hand and squeezed hers. "I apologize."

"As you should," the cashier said, opening the register.

"I wasn't talking to you," he stated.

The woman gasped at the same time Bailey released an exasperated sigh. With a swiftness that reflected her eagerness to remove herself from the premises, the girl grabbed the baby clothes the woman had rung up. As she shoved the outfit into the bag that held a new dress for her, the cashier slammed his change on the counter.

Matteo shoved his wallet and the cash into his back pocket and grabbed a bag. With his hand on her lower back, he escorted Bailey to the escalator and out of the store.

At the car, he tossed the bag onto the back seat as she continued to glance around while worrying her lip.

Not wanting to stress her, he took her right hand in his left and said, "I'm sorry." He placed his free hand on top, creating a sandwich.

Matteo held his breath as she stared at their appendages. He prayed she wasn't offended by his actions and insist on finding her own way to the hospital. For the first time in months, he was enjoying himself and wasn't ready to call an end to the day.

A second passed before Bailey raised her head and smiled.

Like yawns, smiles were contagious. A grin spread across his face until his cheeks ached. "How are the pains?"

"The same," she replied.

"Still thirty minutes apart?"

"About twenty." Her voice shook.

"How 'bout we get the tags off these purchases and pack your bag? Afterwards, we can head over to Woolworth's for a cola."

Matteo retrieved a six-inch switchblade from the glove compartment to remove the sales tags and watched as Bailey examined each item before neatly folding it into the suitcase. When she had finished packing, they headed to the five-and-dime store, where he treated them to chicken salad sandwiches and soda.

They ate, chatted, and laughed like old friends until

her pauses during the replies to his questions became more frequent. Recognizing it was time, Matteo drove Bailey to the hospital. He helped her out of the car and carried her bag into the medical facility.

"Miss Collins would like to check in," Matteo announced when they reached the admission desk.

"Of course." The nurse behind the desk smiled as she paged an orderly.

"You'll be okay," Matteo insisted.

"You're not coming with me?" Bailey asked.

"Sorry, only mothers are allowed in the delivery rooms," a second nurse replied as she entered the lobby behind the orderly, pushing a wheelchair. "But we'll take care of you."

Matteo handed the nurse the suitcase. "They're good here." When he turned back to Bailey, she was holding out two singles.

"This is all I have," she said. "I'll get the rest to you over time."

He took her hand in his, closed her fingers over the bills and shook his head. "Your money's no good here, Shorty."

Without warning, Bailey threw her arms around his neck. Caught off guard, Matteo held his hands out.

"Thank you," she whispered.

A lump grew in the back of his throat. His arms slowly wrapped around her and, for a heartbeat it was just the two of them. There were no onlookers who disapproved because of the differences in their race, financial status, and education. No nagging wives. And no absent fathers who would never know the sweet sound of their baby's coo.

All too soon, she pulled back and placed a chaste

kiss on his cheek. Her demonstration of gratitude was brief, yet when her arms dropped to her side, Matteo felt a void neither a bottle of the bar's best nor a meaningless fling would fill.

Chapter One

May 27, 1959

Norma Collins had a big mouth.

Minutes after her birth, the girl's shrieks pulled Bailey from a drug-induced sleep. From that day on, the child used only two volumes…loud and louder.

Norma's ability to project her voice to the back of an auditorium earned her the role of the narrator in several school performances. It alerted babysitters to the direction she ran off when playing outside. And it helped Bailey pinpoint the location of her cheering squad in the room filled with hundreds of other spectators gathered for the graduation ceremony.

Bailey waved at the four-foot girl, sitting on the shoulders of Nicholas Santiano three rows behind the seats reserved for the graduates. For all the nights she had to go to bed before her mother got home from class and the Saturdays she had to sit in the hall at the college with a coloring book, Norma deserved to walk across the stage. Not surprisingly, the school administrators balked when Bailey made the request. They had allowed a single mother to attend classes; they were not about to shine a spotlight on her status.

"Bailey Elizabeth Collins."

Her uncle's cheers competed with Norma's to drown out the announcer's amplified voice. Nicholas's high-pitched whistles joined the ovations.

Bailey marched across the stage to the president of the college. The smile on his thin lips reached up to his gray eyes as she moved the yellow tassel on her maroon cap from the right to the left. He offered his congratulations as he passed her the rolled-up diploma and shook her hand.

Bailey returned the smile and thanked the man who acted as a voice for students who received grades that did not match what was deserved. His intervention had helped reverse an F a professor gave her during her freshman year to discourage her from pursuing a degree in accounting. Thankfully, her incentive for achieving was stronger than the professor's determination to hold her back.

She released the man's hand and stepped in front of the grim-faced dean, who had not reconciled to the idea of women attending college. For four years, she had been forced to listen to his lectures on women not knowing their place before he reluctantly approved her courses for the next term.

He grimaced as if he wanted to spit on her outstretched hand instead of shaking it. "I bet you're proud of yourself."

Bailey's grin grew wider. Of course she was proud of herself. Six years earlier, her daughter had gotten down on her hands and knees in front of the family, mimicked scrubbing the kitchen floor, and proudly announced she wanted to grow up to be like her mother.

The innocent act had reminded Bailey of the dreams she had placed on the back burner when she learned she was pregnant. It also made her realize she had to be more than the breadwinner and caregiver. She needed to be a role model, too.

"Yes, I am," Bailey's replied, standing tall in the ankle-length maroon gown that symbolized the hard work she'd put in to earn her moment on the stage.

The dean muttered a word that compared her to a female dog as he grabbed her hand and squeezed it hard.

He winced in pain as the jewel she had turned towards the inside of her palm dug into his hand. A gasp from the front row confirmed his second curse reached beyond Bailey's ears. The eyes of everyone in hearing distance locked on them. The president cut short his praise to the next graduate. The administrators seated at the rear of the stage frowned, denoting their displeasure.

The man snatched back his hand and jerked his head towards the steps leading from the stage. Having achieved another goal, Bailey returned to her seat.

"There were rumors the dean crushed the hands of all the women," a young lady whispered as she settled into the seat on Bailey's left. "But he barely touched mine."

Bailey opened her hand and revealed the emerald-and-diamond ring Nicholas's grandmother had lent her. "Hopefully, he'll think twice before he tries it again."

The woman threw her head back and screeched. Her body shook with laughter.

Two men in the row ahead of them glanced over their shoulders. One shushed her. The other raised an eyebrow at Bailey, silently asking to be let in on the joke.

The woman closed her mouth, yet her laughter refused to be contained. She snorted as she wiped the tears from her freckled cheeks. Bailey shook her head and shrugged. The men rolled their eyes and faced forward.

Bailey sat back and laid her black patent leather

purse on her lap. She slipped the ribbon from the diploma, unrolled the scroll, and traced a finger over the carefully printed letters that spelled out her name.

After she decided to return to school, she had purchased two frames and hung them on the wall by the door. She looked forward to finally filling the second frame and hanging it next to her high school diploma.

As the final graduate strutted away from the stage, the president stepped up to the microphone and offered his best wishes to those who were preparing for the next stage in their lives. His last syllable was still echoing through the auditorium when the graduates jumped to their feet and tossed their caps into the air.

Having secured her cap with hairpins, Bailey did not join in the tradition. She watched the upward flight of the mortarboards, then stepped to the side when the man to her right lunged forward to catch his headgear.

While the graduates were celebrating, the Grand Marshal led the faculty and administrators off the stage. As they proceeded up the aisle, Bailey felt someone watching her. It had not been uncommon for people, in awe of a colored woman attending—not cleaning up after—the classes, to stare as she walked around the campus. Most of the time, she ignored the gawkers. But there were occasions she could not help but make eye contact and offer them a smile that informed them she was aware of their scrutiny.

Her gaze moved past the graduates, who beamed with pride, and the bored spectators, anxious to exit the stifling auditorium. Eager to make their way to their various celebratory feasts, no one maintained eye contact for more than a second.

Bailey was resigning herself to the futility of her

search when she spotted him next to the far-right door at the rear of the room. Blue eyes—the eyes that calmed her when she was stressed, teased her until her frown turned upside down and twinkled when her spirits were up—held her gaze. A lock of his wavy chestnut hair brushed his brow. The right corner of his lips pushed up and a dimple split a two-inch scar…a memento from the day his father slammed a fist into his face before disowning him.

Bailey's heart skipped a beat.

What the hell was Matteo doing there? Did he enjoy staring at the world through two black eyes, eating his food through a straw, and losing the use of his limbs?

Knowing Nicholas, if he discovered his cousin, all three ailments would plague Matteo, and no one would step in to stop him.

A throat cleared, alerting Bailey to the empty space in front of her. She hurried forward and stepped into the aisle. Thanks to the congestion at the main exit, she was able to take one more glance to her right.

Her shoulders drooped at the sight of the empty doorway. She would have enjoyed spending the day with the person who had cheered her on during her journey from high school dropout to college graduate, but thanks to his sins, she was the only person present who would welcome him with open arms.

Bailey inched her way into the foyer crowded with bodies that had not been able to squeeze into the auditorium during the ceremonies and the graduates who stopped to search for loved ones. Unable to tolerate the mixture of cigarette smoke, sweet perfume, musky aftershave, and body odor in an unventilated space, she pushed through the crowd until she was standing outside inhaling the fragrant foliage sprouting from the trees and bushes surrounding the campus.

She opened the robe, and a warm breeze brushed across her upper chest. While proud of the gown, Bailey questioned whether the makers had considered the possible heat and humidity when choosing the thick fabric to create academic regalia that would be worn in the late spring.

A bead of perspiration rolled down her back, yet Bailey opted to wait until she reached the car before removing the robe. Everyone insisted her midnight-blue dress was stylish and sophisticated. But without the matching short-sleeved jacket, which she had removed so as not to overheat in the robe, the thin straps that kept her bodice in place made her feel exposed.

"There she is." Norma's scream was the only warning Bailey got before the girl slammed into her. "I'm proud of you, Mommy."

Bailey had thought the happiest moment of her life had been the first time she held her daughter in her arms. Norma's declaration knocked that day to second place.

She embraced the girl as Nicholas and Georgia weaved through the crowd, with her uncle taking up the rear. The older man beamed with the same pride she saw on his face when his daughter graduated two years earlier.

"Congratulations." Georgia Santiano kissed her cheek. "Here's a little something for you." The thickness of the envelope pressed into Bailey's hand suggested there was more than a "little something" inside.

"These are for you." Her uncle held out a bouquet of white roses. "I'm also proud of you. I never thought…" He shook his head and left the sentence unfinished.

There was no need for him to finish the sentence. She was aware many people had believed she would never graduate from high school, much less college. Hell, there were occasions she'd questioned her ability to achieve her goal.

Some nights, no matter how many times she went over a problem, the numbers refused to add up correctly. Then there were concepts she struggled to get straight no matter how many times she reviewed them. And there were the instances when she dozed off in class while her professors went off on a tangent that was nowhere related to the question asked by a student.

A tug on her hand turned her attention to Norma, her inspiration to continue when she struggled. "Can I see it?"

"Tonight." After she placed the diploma in the frame, she would give her daughter a chance to examine it up close before she hung it up. She held the bouquet out. "You want to carry these for me, Busy Bee?"

Never one to pass up an opportunity to be of some assistance, Norma cradled the flowers in her arms as she skipped down the grass-lined walk.

"What happened back there?" Georgia asked as she slipped a freshly manicured brown hand into Nicholas's battered appendage. Though he'd stopped running numbers after he proposed to his wife, he was occasionally called upon to help his father settle disputes, the latest of which involved a man who kept mistaking his child for a punching bag.

"Dean Kurry didn't enjoy having a stone dig into his palm," Bailey replied.

"I preferred my plan," Nicholas said. He appeared oblivious to the passersby whose glares suggested they did not approve of the mixed-race couple. Yet all it would take was one off-color comment for Nicholas to inform the gawkers it would be in their best interest—and health—to mind their own business.

"Thank you, but I couldn't let you accept the diploma on my behalf," Bailey replied to his previous suggestion of walking across the stage and breaking the other man's hand. "There are some battles I need to fight myself."

"I wasn't referring to him," Georgia clarified as her fingers traced small circles over her extended stomach. "During the recessional, it looked like you were staring at someone?"

If her cousin had seen who she'd been staring at, the woman would have mentioned Matteo by name. The knowledge, however, did not settle the jitters in Bailey's stomach. The beating he received before his family disowned him was nothing compared to what they would do if he did not honor the mandate to stay away.

"I thought I saw someone I know," Bailey explained.

Technically, she had not lied. She had seen someone she knew; she just had no intention of revealing his identity.

"If you want to say hi, we'll wait."

Did she want to say hi? Of course, she did.

Just as it took a village to raise a child, it also took a support system for someone to succeed, and Matteo had been there for her from the beginning.

So the real question should be whether she was going to say hi. And the answer would be a resounding, *Hell no*. After everything he had done for her, she could not repay him by alerting the three people on the campus who would least likely appreciate his presence.

"It's fine. We can catch up another time."

They strolled around the corner, where Norma waited by the red convertible that was Nicholas's pride and joy. He opened the door and pushed the front seat forward. The girl climbed into the back and plopped down in the center. Bailey followed her daughter as her uncle walked around and climbed into the back from the driver's side.

"What's next on that list of yours?" Her uncle asked, referring to the list she had written and hung on the refrigerator the day she decided changes were called for.

"Find another job," she replied, thinking of the hardest challenge facing her.

During the commencement ceremony, Bailey could not feign interest in speeches that offered false hope to a quarter of the graduates. The world might be full of possibilities, but only for those of the approved color and with the approved appendages between their legs.

"Nicholas, stop pawing your wife and pay attention to where you're going," Bailey said when he drove straight through the intersection.

"What makes you think I don't know where I'm going?" he asked without removing his hand from his wife's knee.

"You missed the turn, for one thing," Bailey replied, pushing back the jealousy that threatened to consume her whenever she watched the couple, who could not keep their hands to themselves for more than a minute when they were in the same room. There was always a soft brush of a finger against a cheek, a clasp of a hand around another, or the gentle touch on a back.

"Who said I missed anything?"

"Nicholas Santiano—"

"Stop teasing her, Nick." Georgia peered over her shoulder and winked at Norma. "You want to tell her?"

Bailey glanced from her cousin's mischievous grin to her daughter's Shirley Temple curls that bobbed up and down with her head. "Tell me what?" she asked.

"We're throwing you a surprise party," Norma announced loud enough for the people on the sidewalk to stare at them. "Surprise!"

Indeed, the celebration was a surprise. When Bailey invited her uncle and cousin to the graduation, she had also offered to cook dinner for them afterwards. Uncle James insisted he would need to get back to his bar and Georgia offered her apologies, claiming she and Nicholas would have to head to the restaurant they owned to prepare for the evening crowd.

"I'm surprised you didn't suspect something when Little Miss Information asked if she could visit Celeste." Georgia wiggled her fingers at Norma, who burst into a fit of giggles though the woman was more than three feet from her.

Bailey recalled the question Norma had posed when they climbed into the car that morning. Believing the girl was referring to another day, she had told her they would discuss it later.

Before Bailey could express her gratitude, a driver cut off Nicholas. She spent the remainder of the ride trying to distract her daughter from his uncensored grumbles of displeasure.

"Mommy, can I go next door?" Norma asked as Nicholas pulled up in front of the brownstone he and Georgia had moved into when they returned from their honeymoon twelve months earlier. While some would have preferred to put some distance between generations and settle in another part of the city—or, at least, a few blocks away—Georgia had insisted they purchase the house next to her in-laws. But then again, she had practically grown up in the house that belonged to Marcos Santiano, a "financier" who assisted, for a nice return, those the banks snubbed, amongst other activities not considered legal.

"You don't want to celebrate with me?" Bailey asked.

"No, I wanna play with Cousin Celeste's dolls."

Bailey admired the girl's honesty. If given the choice between playing with dolls or hanging with adults, she also would have chosen the toys when she was younger.

"It's all right," Nicholas said. "Celeste is upstairs. She'll keep an eye on her."

His sister being home was not news to Bailey. Since the beating that put her in the hospital two years earlier, the woman rarely went anywhere. Instead of perusing the racks at Bergdorf Goodman, enjoying meals at the Waldorf Astoria, or catching matinees on Broadway, she attended classes at the community college and took care of the house for her grandmother and father.

Bailey did not want to impose on the woman, who had not only lost her unborn child during the attack from her husband but lost the ability to conceive another. The last thing she wanted was to flaunt Norma in front of her.

"Celeste adores your daughter," Nicholas insisted. "Besides, the company will be good for her."

"Please, Mommy." Norma's plea included the puppy-dog eyes that made Bailey roll her own.

A movement shifted her gaze to the woman who

stepped into the doorway of the building next door to her cousin's. Celeste pressed her lips together until they formed a thin line, which for this woman was considered a wide grin. "She can come over."

Assuming Celeste would not have offered her services if she did not mean it, Bailey nodded. "Go ahead, but behave yourself."

"I will, Mommy." Norma scrambled across the seat, sprang out of the car, and raced up the steps to the house.

"Come on." Georgia hooked her arm around Bailey's and led her up the steps to the house that was a big step up from the one-bedroom apartment she had grown up in.

Outside, nothing set the four-story building apart from the other brownstones on the block. All had been built in the nineteenth century. The front yards were enclosed by black wrought iron gates. The same material had been used to fashion the banisters on either side of the steps leading from the street to the parlor level. And acanthus-inspired brackets framed the front doors. Inside, the furniture was sleek and brightly colored, differentiating them from their neighbors, who preferred large, dark-colored pieces.

On the third level, they headed down the blue carpeted hallway. "This is the baby's room," Georgia said, opening the second door on the right.

Bailey stepped into the pale-yellow room. A white crib, dresser, and changing table sat on the plush lime-green wall-to-wall carpet.

"Papa Santiano got me this." Georgia caressed the cherrywood rocking chair next the window covered by green curtain. "And Daddy dropped that off yesterday." She pointed to the rocking horse sitting in the corner by the closet.

At the rate the grandfathers were going, there would be nothing left in the stores for the baby shower two weeks from Saturday.

While they tended to solve problems with their fists and were involved in less than legal activities, the Santianos were known for their generosity. They, particularly Matteo, had welcomed her into their homes when her own family turned their backs on her. And neither Norma nor she ever wanted for anything.

"Have you picked out names?"

"Giorgio if it's a boy and Nicolette if it's a girl," Nicholas stated, stepping into the room.

The play on Nicholas and Georgia's names sounded like something the man would come up with.

"According to Nick, it only seemed right to name the children after us, since his daughter would be a daddy's girl and our son a momma's boy," Georgia elaborated, confirming Bailey's suspicions.

"At least I'm honest," he replied, encircling his arms around his wife.

Nicholas would be tough on his son to ensure the boy was prepared to fulfill his responsibilities as a man, and he would spoil his daughter, giving her everything her heart desired. Georgia, however, would be tough on the girl to make certain her daughter grew up to be a strong, independent woman, but she would coddle the boy to bring out his gentler side.

"Yes, but you didn't have to be so smug about it when we told our fathers."

Bailey silently disagreed as she stared at the mirror image—sans the scar—of Matteo. Nicholas could not help but be smug. It was a trait all the men in the Santiano family shared. One that both infuriated and attracted her to the man who tested her loyalty to the same family who had opened their hearts and home to her.

Chapter Two

"*Te l'avevo detto*." Matteo chuckled. "I told you so."

His grin stretched from ear to ear as he mumbled the sentiment to the empty seat next to him. The driver eyed Matteo in the rearview mirror, while a young mother clutched her toddler to her side and practically scrambled over the seats across the aisle, giving him a wide berth as she headed to the back of the bus.

Despite the other passengers' reactions, Matteo continued to gloat as he replayed Bailey's march across the stage in his mind. He had always believed she would accomplish her dream, even when she worried her lip and pulled at her hair while she struggled with the problems assigned to reinforce the class work. And he had been grateful no last-minute emergencies prevented him from witnessing her shine—or the ugliness that tried to rain in her day.

Matteo rubbed the bruised knuckles on his right hand. For four years he had listened to Bailey recount the lectures the dean gave her about a woman's proper place. Bowing to her wishes, he never visited the educator to let him know what he thought of the man's archaic beliefs. However, all bets were off when the educator referred to her by the vile name instead of congratulating her during what should have been one of her happiest moments.

As the graduates proceeded out of the auditorium,

Matteo stepped into the shadows to avoid being seen by his cousin and further ruining Bailey's day. But the second she rode off with Nicholas and her family, he located the dean's office and demonstrated why the man should not say anything if he had nothing nice to say.

A block away from his stop, Matteo pulled the cord that ran above the windows from the front to the back of the bus. Once the gentle *bing* announced his intentions to disembark, he made his way to the exit at the rear.

The skittish mother warily watched as he headed up the aisle and stopped behind her. She stepped into the rear well; her uneasiness with him outweighed the potential risks of the doors swinging open on their own while the vehicle was still in motion.

The bus pulled up to the curb, and the light over the rear door flashed on. Matteo reached over the mother's shoulder to push the door open. She hopped onto the sidewalk with her son tucked under her arm and sprinted to the corner.

Figuring he needed to tamp down his enthusiasm before everyone in the neighborhood scurried away when he approached, Matteo suppressed the urge to continue saying "I told you so" to the air. He stepped off the bus, turned right, and headed north. Halfway up the block, he jogged across the street and waved to a white-haired, stooped man perched on a crate in front of the candy store, relishing the soft purrs of the cat stretched across the threshold. The pendulum on the clock hanging on the wall behind the counter ticked off a number of seconds before the overenthusiastic chatter of the children who spilled out of the school two blocks away shattered the peace.

Matteo veered left at the corner and strolled to the

four-story apartment building towering over the two-story structure to the right and the empty lot on the left. He picked up a greasy, brown paper bag bouncing down the sidewalk and tossed it into the tin trash can sitting behind the wrought iron fence surrounding the front of the building. After placing the lid back on the can, he jogged up the three steps to the stoop. He turned the brass doorknob, pushed open the glass door, and waited.

No offspring ran up from the basement eager to bombard him with tales of their days. Only silence waited to greet him in the apartment in the lowest level.

Out of all the consequences he suffered for his transgressions, the exile from his family had been the hardest. He had tried to make amends, only to discover that getting clean was easier than getting back into the good graces of his family.

Letters were returned unopened. The dial tone hummed in his ear after the person on the other end heard his voice. And the one time he showed up at his parents' house, he was ordered not to return, before the door was slammed in his face. No excuses were heard or apologies accepted. Not that he blamed them.

It was not like he had not grown up having certain morals drilled into him. Despite the many activities the Santianos were involved with that were frowned upon by the legal system, there were certain codes they followed:

Thou shalt not desecrate thy body with drugs. Thou shalt treat thy woman like a queen. Thou shalt remember children are precious. And thou shalt not steal from family.

Break any of the codes and you were considered dead in the eyes of the family. Break multiple codes or strike a woman or child and the death would be literal.

Matteo squared his shoulders and plowed forward. Despite his aversion to the solitude, he could not walk away. There were chores that needed to be attended to before the day was over.

He was halfway down the steps leading to the basement when a door on the second floor slid across the frame.

"It's only me, Mrs. Murphy," he called to the woman who had appointed herself the unofficial guardian of the building and kept tabs on everyone's comings and goings. He, however, was not sure what the four-foot-eight-inch grandmother could do if she did catch an unsavory character hanging around.

"Who's me?" the woman called.

"Matteo," he replied, jogging up the stairs to reassure the woman.

Mrs. Murphy cracked open the door wide enough for her to peep into the hall. She glanced at the gold watch decorating her wrist, squinted once, then shook her head. Matteo wasn't sure what she was expecting, as the timepiece had not worked in the eighteen months he had lived in the building.

Her devotion to the watch—her late husband had worked two jobs to purchase it for their first anniversary, to make up for the wedding ring he had been unable to give her—reminded Matteo that not every woman was a materialistic shrew like the woman he had the displeasure of marrying. During the years he had been with Eleanor, his wife had been so demanding of his wallet he sometimes wished he had stuck his feet in the path of his mother's broom when she swept the floors.

"Do you have the time?" Mrs. Murphy asked.

He glanced at his watch. "Two-fifty."

"Mr. Patraski was looking for you an hour ago. His window's stuck."

The news came as no surprise to Matteo. He had warned the man not to close the window until the paint on the sill had dried, yet he'd heard the window slam shut as he was leaving for the graduation.

"I'll take a look at it," Matteo replied.

"Good." She nodded her approval. Having passed along the message, she was free to indulge in her next favorite pastime. "So, where did you disappear to today?" Her eyes were alert, eager for news.

"I was attending a graduation." His smile returned as he recalled Bailey's march across the stage to receive her diploma. She had set a goal for herself and refused to let anyone or anything prevent her from achieving it.

"High school?"

"No, college."

Mrs. Murphy beamed with pride. "You know a college graduate?"

"Yes, ma'am."

"Well, why aren't you out celebrating with him?"

"It was a woman," he corrected. Her smile grew wider, and he quickly added, before she could inquire, "There's nothing between us."

"Why not?" Mrs. Murphy's smile faded. "Is she ashamed of you?"

Matteo shook his head. Bailey would never look down her nose on someone for performing manual, and honest, work. "It's family related."

The woman hmphed. "I don't like her," she announced, despite having never met Bailey.

"Actually, you remind me a bit of her." Matteo chuckled. "You're both feisty women." Of course, that was the only thing they had in common.

Besides the difference in age, skin color, and ethnicity, each woman stirred different feelings inside him. Mrs. Murphy reminded him of his grandmother, who commanded respect from each of her sons, grandchildren, and great grands. His feelings for Bailey, on the other hand, were far from chaste.

He had never intended for their relationship to grow beyond that of benefactor and beneficiary. Yet three years earlier, when an innocent peck on the cheek turned into a deep kiss that made him harder than he had ever been, he had been forced to recognize how much she had grown, how different she was now. The scared girl had metamorphized into a beautiful woman capable of igniting a fire in him.

A thunderous racket that could only come from a young man who had been set free of the confines of a classroom interrupted the tranquility of the building. With the sigh of one who had repeatedly reprimanded the youngster for his exuberance, Mrs. Murphy folded her arms over her chest and waited until the red curly tresses appeared over the top step before she asked, "Do you have to make so much noise?"

"Sorry, Gran. I didn't know you were in the hall." Along with the apology, Liam Murphy leaned down and kissed his grandmother's cheek.

The sixteen-year-old had the decency to look contrite. However, Matteo was willing to bet the boy would forget his remorse the next time he encountered a flight of stairs.

A week after Matteo took over the maintenance of the building, Mrs. Murphy had ventured down to the basement to welcome him. The conversation quickly shifted to Liam, whose father had died when he was ten and grandfather passed on six months later. She went on to discuss the importance of children having role models in their lives.

Taking the not-so-subtle hint, Matteo occasionally asked the boy to help around the building, then listened as the teen grumbled about problems young people considered important but would mean nothing to him in ten years.

"What's with the cool threads?" Liam gave Matteo the onceover.

Two years ago, a white shirt and black pants purchased off the sales rack would not have been considered special. Matteo used to have suits made simply for hanging out at bars. But then, he also spent more time away from home, trying to find happiness at the bottom of a glass and at the end of a rolled-up bill.

"He went to a college graduation," Mrs. Murphy said. "Hopefully, I'll get to attend one someday."

Liam glanced towards Matteo, his eyes begging him to deflect the upcoming lecture. He understood the youngster's pain—the last thing he wanted to hear was a speech from his grandmother when he was that age. Still, he shook his head.

The little shit needed to be grateful he had someone who gave a damn about him. And maybe if just one of the woman's lectures sank in, Liam would be spared the pain of learning life's lessons the hard way.

"Matteo, help," a voice called from the top floor.

He headed up the steps as a pair of slippers slapped against the marble floor. A young brunette, who had not taken the time to change out of her floral housedress or remove the curlers from her hair, met him on the landing between the third and fourth floor.

"What's wrong?"

"I'm having a little problem with my toilet." She held her index finger and thumb close together.

"I'll be up in a minute."

"Thank you," the woman replied as she skipped back up the steps.

"Need help?" Liam asked when Matteo returned to the second floor.

Knowing the offer was made to get away from the lecture, Matteo shook his head again. "No, I got it."

The boy mouthed, *Thanks a lot*, before shuffling past his grandmother into the apartment.

Matteo headed back downstairs, past the postman on the first level, and to the basement. He pushed open his door and stepped into the apartment that, depending on the person's perspective, was either a testament to how far he had fallen or a demonstration of his willingness to accept the consequences of his actions.

As a child, Matteo would listen in awe as his grandmother described the two-room Lower East Side attic apartment she and her husband lived in after they arrived in America. The family made do until their sons grew up and established businesses that would ensure the next generation had more.

While many of the activities would get the men five to ten years if they were caught, his grandmother had been proud of her sons' successes and was not against her grandchildren continuing the tradition. Yet instead of learning the family business, Matteo had been too busy chasing highs that promised euphoria but delivered chaos.

By the time his eyes were opened, he was without

family and living in an apartment smaller than the living room in his previous house.

Realizing a trip to Pityville would neither earn him sympathizers nor fix the toilet, Matteo pulled the chain dangling over the card table in the center of the room that served as his living room, kitchen and dining room. The furniture, which had been abandoned by the previous superintendent, had been in decent enough condition that Matteo decided to keep it instead of purchasing more modern pieces.

He stepped into the bathroom to the left and exchanged the suit for the brown twill pants and tan shirt hanging on the back of the door. After too many bruised shins to keep track of, he'd learned how to maneuver in the two-foot-wide space between the tub and wall. He just wished he could remember during his bathroom runs in the middle of the night to duck when he passed under the low-hanging light in the bedroom.

Matteo tossed his shirt into the sink to soak and hung his pants on the back of the door. He then went back to the other room and grabbed his toolbox from the top of the sideboard next to the bedroom.

His stomach growled as he headed out the door, reminding him he had not eaten since nine that morning. The immediate tasks should not take more than ten to fifteen minutes to complete. After he finished, he could fix himself a sandwich before tackling the rest of his chores.

Matteo stopped at the rear apartment on the fourth floor and knocked on the door. He waited the twelve seconds it took for the woman to answer.

She held the newest addition to her household against her left shoulder. The diaper protecting her housedress was stained with the milk the baby had ejected when he burped. A boy, no older than two, stood behind her sucking on the fore and middle fingers of his right hand.

"Thank you for coming." She stepped aside and waved him into the apartment.

There was a splash when his right foot came down over the threshold. His gaze dropped to the growing puddle and followed it to the bathroom, where the water covered the floor. He rushed to the room. The remains of a complete roll of toilet paper floated on the top of the bowl as water ran over the side.

Sighing, he mentally crossed eating anytime soon from his to-do list.

Chapter Three

"You're back for more cake?" Sophie Santiano, whom everyone lovingly referred to as Nonna, glanced up from the sausage and peppers she had been spooning from a casserole dish into a sky-blue plasticware bowl.

After the two heaping plates of food and two slices of cake, Bailey could hardly be hungry again that night. Yet one whiff of the hearty dish made her stomach growl.

Regrettably, she had to shake her head at Nonna's inquiry. Having achieved her goals, she needed to focus on helping Norma realize her dreams. The first step towards success was making sure the girl got the sleep necessary to retain what was learned in school.

"No, I've got to get Norma home." Bailey carried her plate to the sink. "She has school in the morning."

"Leave that," Nonna replied when Bailey turned on the hot water.

"I wish you would let me help you clean up," Bailey said, switching off the water instead of risking a wooden spoon across the back of her hand for disobeying the older woman.

Nonna was on the plus side of seventy but still ruled her family with a firm hand. Even the men, who towered over the woman, heeded her commands, as she would not hesitate to crack a knuckle with a utensil or a head with the cane she kept by her side.

"Nonsense, you're the guest of honor." The older woman set the dish aside and snapped the lid on the bowl. "Enjoy having no responsibilities for a day."

Bailey could not remember the last time she had that luxury. Growing up on a farm had her in the fields as soon as she was big enough to carry a sack. Back then, she grumbled at the work expected of her. Little had she known how easy she had it. All she had to worry about was finishing her school assignments and tackling her chores. Rent, utilities, and bills were not a part of her vocabulary.

"Thank you, Nonna." Bailey kissed the older woman's cheek, then started towards the kitchen door. A glint of sparkle near her side reminded her of the ring she had borrowed. "I forgot to give this back to you." She slipped the jewelry from her finger. "It worked as you predicted."

Bailey explained the dean's surprise when the gem dug into his palm and his reluctance to shake the other woman's hand. She did omit the expletive the man muttered, so as not to upset the woman.

"I'm glad everything worked out for you." Nonna wrapped her hand around Bailey's. "You keep it. It's a graduation gift."

No, a graduation present was a pen, or a dollar or two to help her purchase what she would need for her new career. It was not an heirloom the elderly woman had inherited from an aunt. "It's too much."

"After all your hard work, you deserve it," Nonna said. "Don't argue with an old woman," she added, lightly tapping Bailey's hand with a spoon. "It's not good for your health."

Chuckling, Bailey slipped the ring back on her

finger. "Thank you," she replied, hugging the woman.

"Now, go get your little one home so we'll have another graduation to celebrate in fourteen years."

Bailey ran up to the fourth level, which Celeste Santiano had always called home, except for the few weeks she had been married to her childhood crush. Norma's voice directed her mother to the playroom overlooking the garden. The toys Celeste had once dreamed of passing down to her own daughter filled the room.

Two porcelain dolls lay on a pillow at the head of the bed, while stuffed animals of various shapes and sizes occupied a rocking chair near the foot. A model train set that used to belong to Nicholas sat on the floor underneath the window. And books ranging from early readers to classic literature filled a corner bookshelf.

"What do you have there, Busy Bee?" Bailey asked, pushing away from the door frame she had leaned against while Norma finished reading the chapter in the book she held in both hands.

"Nancy Drew." Norma closed the book and turned the cover to her mother. "It's about a sixteen-year-old detective who's trying to help some friends."

"Does she succeed?"

Norma shrugged. "I don't know. I just started reading the book."

"If you want, you can take it home and finish it," Celeste said.

"Really?"

"Yes."

Norma threw her arms around the woman's neck. "Thank you, Cousin Celeste."

"You need to go downstairs and say goodbye to

everyone," Bailey announced. "You have school in the morning."

Hugging the book to her chest, Norma slid off the green settee and raced out of the room. The carpet softened the smack of her hard-soled shoes against the steps.

"I should have asked you if it was okay to let her take the book," Celeste said.

"That's fine. It'll save us from having to look for it in the library on Monday. She'll return it when she's finished."

"Take your time." She threw a quick glance at the doll sitting next to the spot Norma vacated. "It's not like I'll need it anytime soon."

Bailey's heart ached for Celeste. Maybe allowing Norma to spend time in the playroom had not been such a good idea.

"I'm sorry—"

"Don't!" Celeste snapped. "If anyone should be sorry, it's whatever Fate thought it'd be funny to curse me with this." She pointed to the red birthmark that covered the left side of her face from her brow to her cheekbone.

The angel's kiss was the only feature on the woman that had not changed over the past two years. While recuperating from the injuries inflicted by her husband, Celeste had cut her long hair into a short, curly style that barely brushed her collar. She'd also cleared her closet of the fashionable clothes she previously favored, giving several of the more expensive outfits to friends and relatives, including the dress Bailey wore for the graduation. They were replaced with plain cotton dresses rivaled only by a nun's habit for dullness.

The most drastic changes occurred in Celeste's once-vibrant expressions. The bright spark in her blue eyes had faded to a dark skepticism and her contagious smile was replaced with a brooding frown.

No matter how hard she tried to downplay her looks, Celeste had an inner beauty that outshined the birthmark and frumpy attire. Others just needed to recognize what the woman's family and close friends saw.

"There's nothing wrong with—"

"You and Georgia are so alike. She's always telling me there's nothing wrong with my face, that it'll take someone special to appreciate me." Celeste snorted. "More like someone who's blind." The woman pushed up from the sofa and snatched up the doll. "I appreciate the kind words. However, I've resigned myself to the fact that I have a face only a mother can love."

Bailey did not share the same closeness with Celeste as Georgia did, but it still hurt to see the woman's misery. She wished Marcos Santiano had not felt the need to dispose of his son-in-law after the abuse was discovered. Gianni Acardis had gotten off easy. For the mental, emotional and physical hurt he'd inflicted upon his wife, he deserved to live a long and *painful* life.

"Thank you for watching Norma." Bailey hugged her cousin's friend. "If you ever need anything…"

Celeste nodded. "Thank you." She returned the hug with a quick embrace before pulling back. She turned to the bed and laid the doll between the other two.

Downstairs, Bailey accepted several bowls of leftovers from Nonna before stepping out front, where her uncle and Norma waited in the car.

"Where's Georgia?" she asked Nicholas, who held the door open for her.

"She's had a long day. I told her to rest," he replied as she climbed into the back seat with her daughter. "I'll be back in about an hour."

Bailey understood that was Nick-speak for the certainty that as soon as they dropped off her uncle, he was going to race through the streets as if the devil was chasing Little Nick with a dull knife. At least he was not reckless like his cousin.

When alcohol and weed no longer calmed the demons plaguing him, Matteo had switched to harder drugs that made him reckless. With no concerns about traffic regulations, he would cut off other drivers—regardless of how big their vehicles were—force pedestrians to jump out of his way, and acted as if stop signs were suggestions.

His behavior finally forced Bailey to refuse his offers for a ride. She had preferred to walk rather than exit his car shaking from the experience.

After they dropped off her uncle in front of his bar, Norma climbed over the seat to claim the space he'd vacated. Nicholas pulled away from the curb and adhered to the speed limit, displaying a remarkable amount of patience as he followed the slow driver in front of him.

"Georgia was thinking about cutting back on her work after the baby's born," he announced as he stopped for the light he would have made if he had gone around the other car. "She'll continue handling the records for the restaurants, but we'll need someone to take over the books at the stores."

Georgia had started keeping the books at the legal businesses owned by the Santianos when an audit revealed Matteo and another cousin had been redirecting funds to fuel their drug habits.

Bailey had cried after she had been informed of Matteo's misdeeds. Whenever she felt it was just her against the world, he would reassure her that she was not alone. But when his world was falling apart, there was nothing she could do about it.

The Santianos had their rules. They would hear no excuses. Accept no apologies. And offer no second chances.

"Did Georgia put you up to this?" Bailey wondered if her cousin really needed to cut back on her work or if they were using the excuse to give her a job.

"You don't believe me," Nicholas said.

"No, I don't," Bailey replied.

Norma glanced up from the petal she had been stroking. "Why don't you believe him?"

Her habit of asking questions had led to more than one elder lecturing Bailey on the evils of allowing the girl to speak when not spoken to. Certain the girl would listen to the conversation whether she was invited or not, Bailey preferred that Norma ask questions and get straight answers instead of drawing her own conclusions.

"'Cause she's a smart woman," Nicholas replied to Norma before confessing to Bailey, "Georgia doesn't want you to have to deal with the same frustrations she faced after graduating."

Bailey recalled her cousin's stories about interviews with men who did not believe a woman could add one plus one, much less calculate the daily receipts for a business. A few times she was subjected to interviewers who simply looked at the color of her skin and pointed her to the broom closet.

"Thank you for the offer," Bailey said. "I'll think

about it." She reached over the seat and patted Norma's shoulder. "You having fun picking at my flowers?"

"I was playing 'he loves me, he loves me not,'" Norma replied. "But I wasn't pulling off the petals."

"Who's this boy you want to love you?" Nicholas asked.

"Michael Cates. His sister's in my class."

"What class is he in?"

"He's in the fifth grade."

Nicholas frowned and Bailey prayed Georgia was carrying a boy. Any female born in the family would have to deal with an overprotective father, who would interrogate any boy who dared to glance in his daughter's direction.

"You can't find any boys your own age?" he asked.

"Eww. They're icky." Norma scrunched up her face. "One of the boys in my class used to hit me on the back of my head when he walked by my desk. I told the teacher, and she said he probably likes me, but I didn't like it."

"The teacher didn't do anything?" Nicholas's eyes narrowed.

"The principal called me in after Norma slapped him with her textbook," Bailey added, to stave off any intervention he felt was necessary. "They wanted to suspend her for three days, but I told him if it was permissible for the boy to express his interest by hitting my baby, then they should have no problem with Norma expressing her disinterest in kind."

"Did the boy stop?" Nicholas asked

"Yes." Norma's head bobbed up and down.

"Remember—love's not supposed to hurt." Nicholas's tone became more serious when he added,

"And never believe you should settle 'cause no one else will come along."

"Um...okay?" Norma glanced back at her mother and raised both eyebrows.

Suspecting he was addressing her and not her daughter, Bailey locked eyes with Nicholas in the rearview mirror. His concern was unmistakable.

Since learning of Celeste's abuse at the hands of her husband, Nicholas had been more attentive to the women in his life. Bailey, however, did not understand why the concern extended to her.

She was not a member of the Santiano family. Not that she did not appreciate spending time with them. They filled the void created when her parents sent her to New York, with no invitation to return to their farm, after she became pregnant. However, when it came right down to it, no agreements had been made between her father and Mr. Santiano to protect her like Georgia.

Her desire for clarification was placed on hold when Norma faced forward and pointed to the man leaning against the black hearse parked halfway down the block Nicholas turned onto. "It's Mr. Winters," she announced in the event Bailey missed the six-feet-six-inches tall, broad-shouldered man with the dark complexion.

Bailey gently tapped her daughter's arm. Norma dropped her hand in her lap.

As the car moved past the hearse, a short blonde bouffant caught Bailey's attention. Until she met the woman, Bailey had never thought a colored could get away with sporting the lighter tresses, but she had to admit it worked well with her neighbor's caramel complexion.

Nicholas pulled up in front of the hearse. With a coy

grin and a wave of her hand, her neighbor sashayed around the black car and across the street. The woman's full hips swayed from side to side, and her overdeveloped chest bounced up and down, capturing the attention of the men strolling past.

To Kyle Winters' credit, he did not offer the seductress a second glance. He pushed away from the hearse and stepped towards the convertible. Before his large hand grasped the handle, Norma shoved open the door and hopped out onto the sidewalk. His gaze darted from the girl to Bailey, who shook her head at her daughter's less than ladylike behavior.

"What's doing?" Kyle nodded at Nicholas as he folded the seat forward.

"Hangin' in there."

"Thank you for the ride," Bailey said as she climbed out of the car. "We'll talk soon."

"Sure," Nicholas replied.

Kyle pushed back the seat and closed the door. The tires squealed as Nicholas sped away from the curb.

"Uncle James gave Mommy flowers." Norma held up the bouquet.

"Sweet," Kyle replied. "And what did you get her?"

"I drew her a picture and bought her candy."

"The picture's going in my memory box," Bailey added.

Norma's wide grin spread at the announcement. Only cherished mementos like her first shoes, her dedication outfit, and the paperweight she made from a rock were stored in the box.

"Mommy also got a diploma," Norm said.

"Impressive," Kyle said. "Maybe one day you'll get one."

"In order to do that, you need to get some sleep, so you'll be alert in school," Bailey said.

Norma held up the book she had borrowed from Celeste. "Can I read another chapter first?"

"That depends on how long it takes for you to get ready for bed," Bailey replied.

Norma waved goodbye to Kyle before skipping towards the garden entrance of the brownstone.

Kyle's hand rested on Bailey's waist.

"Congratulations on graduating." He placed a chaste kiss on her cheek. "How was the ceremony?"

"Long," Bailey replied, trying to ignore the hearse While she respected the man for making an honest living, the reminder of who he worked with gave her the jitters.

"Sorry I couldn't attend, but—"

"I know you had to work." Bailey would never make him choose between her and his job. She could not pay his rent if he was fired for taking off to spend time with her.

"I got something for you." Kyle pulled a blue velvet box from the pocket of his black slacks and lifted the lid.

The gold heart and chain resting on the cushion took Bailey's breath away. Except for the small hoop earrings Georgia had given her as a high school graduation present, she did not wear jewelry—though not for a lack of interest, but simply a shortage of funds for the extravagance.

Had she been a full-time day student like her cousin, she would have only had to pay for textbooks and the bus fare to school. As an evening student, she was forced to fork over three hundred a year for her studies. But in the end, she believed it was worth every penny.

"This is beautiful." She turned and he draped the

necklace around her. "Thank you."

"How 'bout I take you out for a drink to celebrate?" he suggested as he secured the clasp.

"I'd love to, but it's a school night," Bailey replied, facing him.

Lines creased Kyle's forehead. "I thought you were done with classes." He flicked the scroll in her hand.

Bailey waved the diploma at the house. "Norma has school in the morning. I don't go out on a school night."

"I thought that rule was for you."

"No, I need to make sure her homework is completed, her bags are packed, and she's in bed on time." Bailey stroked the thick bicep hidden underneath his white shirt. "We can have drinks on Saturday, like we usually do."

Kyle frowned. He obviously preferred his plan. But instead of vocalizing his displeasure, he nodded.

Bailey would have liked to give him a preview of what he could expect that weekend, but she limited the public displays of affection so as not to contribute to the neighborhood gossip mills. There were too many eyes looking for a show, too many tongues ready to wag, and too many assumptions to be drawn.

Softening her tone, Bailey added, "I'll make it up to you." She offered him a coy grin that said she was a woman of her word.

An answering smirk replaced Kyle's frown, and an unmistakable hunger shone in his eye. "Six o'clock, Saturday?"

"You may want to consider purchasing a couple of bottles so we can skip the bar," Bailey suggested.

"I may do that," he replied.

Bailey backed away until her hip grazed the wrought

iron gate in front of the house. She kissed the air before crossing the small yard to the steps leading to the garden apartment.

Inside, the bouquet lay on top of the papers scattered across the coffee table in the living room. A wrinkled white shirt was draped across a chair arm and a pair of gray boxers were balled up on the seat.

Bailey bristled at the mess her brother made before taking off for the bar where he worked nights. When he'd showed up at her door twelve months earlier, claiming he wanted to give the city a try, she had agreed to let him crash on her sofa in the belief the arrangement was temporary—no more than a month or two—and he would keep his section of the living quarters neat.

Sighing, she grabbed her flowers and proceeded through the sliding doors that divided the living room from the bedroom. A second set of doors on the other side of the room opened to the kitchen.

Baily carefully peeled the paper from the bouquet, then one by one added the roses and the baby's breath sprigs to the brass vase of eucalyptus branches on the corner of the oak dresser.

She had moved into the apartment six years earlier with two suitcases of clothes, a frying pan, and three thick quilts to serve as her bed and Norma's crib. Proud of having a place of her own, she had been content to make do with the scant possessions until she saved enough money to purchase more. Yet a week after she had settled in, Matteo had shown up with a truckload of furniture his wife no longer wanted, though they had not owned the pieces long enough for them to be scuffed.

By then he had done so much for her—from helping her find the apartment to driving Norma and her from

Uncle James's home to her new place—that she balked at the gift. But he had stood unflinching until she had finished fussing at him, then asked if she was going to show the movers where to place everything, or should he.

At the time, when he set his mind to something, nothing could sway him. Then again, his presence at her graduation proved little had changed.

When Matteo expressed interest in attending the ceremony, Bailey listed the reasons it was not a good idea. Yet even the threat of a beating from Nicholas had not kept him away.

With the aid of the invisible springs strapped to the bottom of her feet, Norma bounced from the kitchen into the bedroom and onto the bed. The front of her blue, short-sleeved pajama shirt was damp from the rushed prep for bed.

"Did you get any water on your face?" Bailey asked.

"Yes." Norma pushed her face forward. "See."

Up close, she saw the drops of water that had not been wiped from Norma's hairline. It meant an extra five minutes to smooth the girl's edges in the morning.

Bailey opened the top dresser drawer and pulled out a white-and-pink-striped pajama top. She took the two steps to the bed as Norma crawled to the edge. In two quick motions, she pulled the damp shirt over the girl's head and replaced it with the dry one.

"I'm ready for bed," Norma announced as she slipped her arms through the sleeves. "Can I read?"

"Yes, you *may*." Bailey stressed the last word with hopes her little one would one day speak proper English. It amazed her how someone who read as much as her daughter could have such atrocious grammar.

Norma dropped back onto the pillows and picked up the borrowed book from the nightstand. As the child flipped to the last page she'd read, Bailey carried her diploma to the kitchen and carefully placed it in the frame purchased a week earlier.

After numerous nights staring at pages until her vision blurred, taking notes until her fingers cramped, and repeating lessons until she saw them in her sleep, she had achieved her goal. But now she had the degree, and her daughter had been set in the right track, she was not sure where to go from there.

Nicholas's job offer was perfect. The Santianos offered generous compensation packages to their employees, which would enable Bailey to save money to help Norma when she attended college. It would also spare her the months of interviews with managers who did not believe women—or coloreds—could achieve.

The only obstacle was Bailey's uncertainty. Did she have what it took to work with numbers all day, every day, for the next forty years?

Chapter Four

The bell attached to the door announced Bailey's arrival as she rushed into Mama's Kitchen fifteen minutes after her eight o'clock shift had started. She waved to the raven-haired waitress hovering over the second booth from the door, jotting down an elderly couple's order in her notepad. Two men sat at the counter grumbling over their failed attempts to pick up skirts from a nearby bar the previous evening, while a mother tried to divert her toddler's attention from the provocative conversation.

Bailey stepped through the swinging door into the kitchen, where Anita Montello, aka Mama, slid a miniature pancake man onto a plate with two strips of bacon.

"I was beginning to wonder if the college graduate quit on me," Anita said.

"Not a chance," Bailey replied. "That degree won't pay the rent," she added, stepping into the small office to her right and dropping her clear, floral print bag in the gray metal chair by the two-drawered steel desk.

"It'll open doors for you, and when it does, you'll be outta here like that." The woman snapped her fingers.

If that was true, she would not be in an office barely bigger than a broom closet, changing into a pink uniform with white trim. Instead, she would be settling into her own office, working on the books her cousin turned over to her.

Bailey had spent the night thinking about Nicholas's offer and every reason accepting the position would be one of the best moves she could make. Yet when she passed the pay phone on the way to the bus stop, she could not bring herself to stop and make the call.

"It's not that easy," Bailey replied. "It took my cousin months before she found a job."

"That was two years ago. Times are changing."

Bailey disagreed. The dean's comment proved there were plenty who would not accept a woman who wanted to be more than a wife and mother. And the sly glances she received whenever she sat in the front of the bus reminded her of the freedoms others would happily deny her if she was living somewhere other than New York City.

She finished buttoning her uniform, shoved a notepad and pencil into her pocket, and headed into the dining room. The next eight hours were spent running between the kitchen and dining room, serving men who occasionally forgot her derriere was not on the menu, mothers who could not control the fruit of their wombs, and couples who thought nothing of speaking freely about "her kind" as if she was not in the room.

Bailey had thought the Fates had been smiling down on her when she saw the Help Wanted sign in the window days after she decided to follow her dreams. She had calculated that, with tips, she would bring home more than from her previous job. However, she had not considered the daily test of her endurance and patience as she dealt with people who believed she was not worth the energy it would take to turn their eyeballs in her direction when speaking to her.

By the end of her first day, she had been so tired, physically and mentally, she almost broke down when Matteo walked into the diner and announced his intention of driving her home. She had to dig deep to find the strength to walk to the car. Once they arrived at her apartment, she again had to find strength to get from the car to the building.

Thanks to the pep talk he gave her that evening—along with the foot massage—she found it possible to return to the diner the next day.

The support Matteo had provided over the years did not stop her from rolling her eyes at him when he strolled into the restaurant the evening after she graduated and perched on a stool as if he had not tried to court danger the previous day.

She was preparing to scold him for his reckless behavior when he placed a white, tissue-wrapped package on the counter. She glanced from the gift to the man, who held her gaze just as he had done in the auditorium.

"Aren't you gonna say something, Shorty?" Matteo asked.

"Have you lost your ever-loving, cotton-picking mind?" Bailey was certain the question was not what he was hoping for, but it had been the one on the tip of her tongue ever since she became aware of him at the graduation.

He leaned forward and braced his forearms on the edge of the counter. "Last I checked, I had all my faculties."

"You should get a second opinion." She tossed her notepad next to the gift and crossed her arms over her chest. "Something obviously came loose since the last time you checked."

"I told you I wasn't going to miss you walking across that stage," Matteo said.

"And I told you what would happen if Nicholas saw you."

He leaned back and spread his arms wide, showing off a broad chest covered by a black t-shirt. "Obviously he didn't see me."

A woman sitting at the end of the counter inhaled hard and choked on the limeade she had been drinking. The female at the table next to the window dropped her fork as she gaped at Matteo.

Bailey was unfazed by the display. Not that she didn't appreciate his looks; she was just too annoyed by his antics.

She rolled her eyes and replied, "If he did, he would've wiped that cocky grin off your face." She grabbed a clean utensil and passed it to the other waitress. "Was it worth the risk?"

Matteo's smile faded. "Yes." There was enough force behind the one word to assure her he meant it. "The day you announced you were going to college, I promised I'd stick with you 'til the end."

Matteo tweaked her cheek like he had done when he found her sulking on the stoop of his uncle's brownstone after Norma's imitation of Bailey scrubbing the floors.

Instead of celebrating her cousin's high school graduation, she had been mourning her own failure to finish school and set an example for her daughter. Matteo listened while she rambled on about her unfulfilled dreams, and then he encouraged her when she made the decision to return to school.

Not once did his faith in her ability to accomplish

her goal waver. Even when she struggled with her math and wondered if she had what it took.

Matteo tapped the present he placed on the counter. "Open it."

Bailey tore off the paper and lifted the lid from the small box. The black leather handbag appeared similar in style to one she had seen in a catalog for an upscale department store in the city. Upon further examination of the exterior design, she realized it truly *was* the same handbag.

She opened the clasp, peeped inside, and shook her head. In addition to spending twenty-five dollars for the bag, Matteo had tucked a white embroidered handkerchief and gloves in the main pocket. A compact mirror rested in a smaller pocket, and several folded bills peeked from the half-opened zipper pocket.

"This is too much." She repeated the same argument she used to give him whenever he dropped by her apartment bearing gifts to celebrate Christmas, her birthday, or the stars aligning right in the sky.

"It's what every accountant needs when she searches for a job."

During her shift, Bailey had pushed Nicholas's job offer to the back of her mind to focus on the orders. Matteo's comment not only reminded her of the decision she needed to make, but its effect on their friendship.

"Nicholas said Georgia's cutting back on her work when the baby's born. They'll need someone to take over the books for the stores, including your father's," Bailey announced as she placed the purse back into the box.

Matteo pulled a pack of cigarettes from the breast pocket of his shirt. He lit a cigarette and released a cloud of smoke before he said, "You should go for it." There was no trace of malice in his tone.

"It doesn't bother you?" she asked.

He reached across the counter and squeezed her hand. "I'd never stand in your way."

Calluses, formed from the long hours he worked to keep the building he managed comfortable for all the tenants, scratched her. It was a far cry from the smooth hand she'd grasped the day he furnished her apartment. Back then, his skin was only marred by a callus on his right forefinger where his pen rested when he worked.

So much had changed for both of them in six years. Some experiences, like her graduation, were cause for celebrating, while others, like the loss of his family, were mourned. Yet the one thing that remained constant was his unflinching support.

"Are you almost finished here?" Matteo asked.

She turned his arm to glance at his watch. She had made up her time from that morning plus fifteen extra minutes.

"After I take your order."

"I'll take it," Anita announced, stepping into the dining room from the kitchen. "It's getting late. You should get ready to go."

While Anita paid well, she was not keen on paying her employees for more than the forty hours they were scheduled to work each week. Not that Bailey was eager to put in more hours.

She had gotten used to taking orders from people who barely acknowledged her presence, and she had increased her endurance and no longer wanted to fall flat on her face the second she stepped out of the diner, but she looked forward to quitting time, when she could go home, put up her feet, and listen to Norma ramble on about her day.

Bailey carried the box with her new purse to the office. She changed back into the red-and-white polka-dotted dress she wore that morning and slipped on her black pumps, adding an inch to her height.

Five minutes later, she returned to the dining room with everything packed in her tote bag. When she announced she was ready, Matteo grabbed a container with his dinner and escorted her out of the building.

****

Determined to catch the bus before the light changed, Matteo grasped Bailey's hand and dashed to the stop. They arrived as the opposing light turned yellow.

He knocked on the glass and sighed with relief when the driver opened the doors. They thanked the transit employee as they each deposited a nickel and dime into the farebox.

"What did you do after the ceremony?" Matteo asked, dropping down on the forward-facing seat in the rear of the bus.

Bailey sat back in the window seat next to him. "We had a cookout at your uncle's house."

Matteo closed his eyes and recalled the last Santiano cookout he had attended, two years earlier. The children played in the front of his uncle's brownstone, while the adults lounged around the back yard, enjoying the food spread out on two tables. The hearty aroma of charcoal-grilled meat drifted through the neighborhood, teasing those who had not been lucky enough to score an invitation to the festivities.

Voices rose to be heard over each other. Laughter lifted spirits. And the peace that came from being surrounded by family offered comfort.

Matteo had taken his family for granted. He did not realize what it meant to have people who cared for him—until he was no longer welcomed.

He opened his eyes and stared at the woman who had not turned her back on him. She had offered him another chance, giving him hope that one day others would be willing to open their hearts and homes to him again.

"I wanna take you out to celebrate," Matteo said, pushing aside the melancholy that threatened to consume him. "What are you doing Saturday night?"

"I told Kyle last night I'd see him Saturday."

"You saw Kyle yesterday?"

"He was at the house when I got there." Bailey held up the charm dangling from her neck. "He gave me this."

Matteo had extended his invitation as a friend. After dinner and movie, he expected their evening to end with him placing a chaste kiss on her forehead…far away from her plump lips…and him returning home to the company of his palm. Yet he bristled at the mention of the other man.

His jealousy was unreasonable. As someone considered dead to his family, he could not offer her a relationship that would end in a happily-ever-after. Bailey may not be family, but as the cousin of his cousin's wife, she was close enough to be considered off-limits.

"Maybe we can do something on Sunday," Bailey suggested.

It was not what he wanted, but Matteo was not about to make an all-or-nothing demand. The proposition would backfire, and he would walk away the loser.

Coming up with a solution that would work for everyone, he suggested, "How 'bout I take you and Norma to the zoo?"

"Norma would like that," Bailey said.

"What about Norma's mother? Would she like to go to the zoo, too?"

"I would."

"Then it's a date." Or, as much of a date as he could hope for with Bailey.

"I'll pack sandwiches," Bailey said.

Matteo shook his head at the strategy some people used to save money on an outing. "You're not to worry about a thing." He wanted to go all out for the day, even if it was a simple trip to the zoo.

Bailey pulled the cord to signal their stop. When they climbed off through the back door, Matteo could not help but notice the change in the demographics of her neighborhood. Unlike the area around Williamsburg where she worked, here he was the minor amongst the coloreds, who had settled in Bedford Stuyvesant beginning in the 1800s.

Matteo was under no illusion that everyone accepted him because he was friends with Bailey. A few, like her next-door neighbors, were friendly and exchanged pleasantries with him. Others didn't give him a second glance when he walked down the street. Then there were those who scowled, silently asking why he was invading their neighborhood.

Taking cues from their behavior, Matteo greeted those who welcomed him, he didn't bother anyone who ignored him, and he kept a close eye on the ones who seemed perturbed by his presence. No harsh words were spoken or actions taken, unless Bailey was harassed. At that point, the instigator would learn how much her happiness meant to Matteo.

While Bailey ducked into the corner store, he waited outside to smoke a cigarette and catch up with an older man who lived in the apartment above her and maintained the building. She returned ten minutes later, having fallen victim to the curse of purchasing more items than what she originally went in for.

Matteo pushed away from the wall, tossed his butt into the street, and took the shopping bag from Bailey. They rounded the corner the same moment Norma dashed from the white line drawn across the middle of the street. Despite her pink dress and saddle shoes, she flew past three of the four boys racing with her.

Bailey stopped and sighed. Her head dropped back as if she was looking for strength from a higher power. The pained expression on her face said she was far from impressed by her daughter's decision to run with the boys instead of jumping rope with the other girls.

"I bet *you* beat all the boys when you were younger," Matteo said.

Bailey glared at him over her shoulder. Amused, he cocked an eyebrow.

"I came in second," she admitted. "I could never catch up with Ernie Burns."

"She's simply following in her mother's footsteps," he commented as the girl crossed a second white line on the heels of the winner.

Matteo chuckled when she rolled her eyes at him.

"How's my Busy Bee?" she said, embracing the girl who had run to them.

"I scraped my knee in the yard during recess." Norma released her mother and stuck out her right leg.

The mercurochrome used to disinfect her knee had dyed the various cuts red.

"It doesn't look like the scratch slowed you down," Matteo said.

"But it did." She grimaced at the boy who won the race. "Donald's never beaten me before."

Bailey chuckled. "Who cleaned your knee?"

Norma pointed towards a group of teenage girls sitting on a stoop watching the younger children play. The seventeen-year-old who picked up Norma from school each afternoon waved at Bailey before whispering to her friends. They shyly tossed glances at Matteo while bursting into a fit of giggles.

"Can I take your diploma in for Show and Tell?" Norma asked, walking backwards.

"Why?"

"No one believes you graduated. Albert wonders why anyone would go to school when someone wasn't forcing 'em."

No one had vocalized their doubts in her abilities, but Matteo had seen the skepticism in their eyes when Bailey announced she was going back to school. He suspected some wondered how a single mother would manage to maintain a job, go to school, and care for her daughter. Then there were those who rolled their eyes, silently communicating the belief she would give up, pop out several more children, and then expect the government to help her support them.

Matteo never had any doubts about her achieving. When he glanced in Bailey's eyes, he saw the one thing that would beat skepticism each time—a mother's determination to do for her child.

"You tell him I went back to school for you," Bailey

said. "I wanted to make sure you knew it was an option."

"I don't understand," Norma said.

Bailey patted the girl's head. "You will one day."

The girl shrugged her shoulders, spun around, and skipped to the house. They walked in at the same time Lincoln Collins stepped from the kitchen to the hall, with drops from his recent shower clinging to the chest hairs peeping from his sleeveless undershirt. His half-closed bloodshot eyes gave him the appearance of someone who was waking up after a two-day bender.

"The prodigal brother has returned," Bailey said.

Lincoln walked past her into the living room. "Hey, Sis," he greeted, tossing a beige shirt onto the back of the chair.

"You forgot how to put things away?" She kept on his heels.

"No, I haven't."

"Then I'd appreciate it if this went where it's supposed to go." Bailey snatched up the shirt and tossed it over her brother's head.

Matteo carried the groceries into the kitchen and set them on the table as Bailey ran through the list of chores Lincoln had neglected around the apartment. Norma, who had followed Matteo to the rear of the apartment, dove into the bag. One by one she unpacked the cans and boxes of food and lined them on the counter. The steady drip of water from the faucet distracted him from the arguing siblings.

"How long has this been leaking?" he asked, inspecting the sink.

Bailey's mumbles grew louder as she marched down the hall. She glanced at the sink and rolled her eyes.

"I left you a note to tell Mr. Roberts about that," she

said to her brother, who followed her as far as the threshold.

"I didn't see no note," Lincoln said.

"It was on your pillow."

Her brother sucked his teeth. "Woman, how you expect me to read anythin' when I get in? I can barely focus long enough to move those papers you leave to the coffee table."

Bailey crossed her arms over her chest and turned back to Matteo. "It's been like this a week, and Mr. Roberts was away."

"I'll fix it."

"That's not necessary…at least it wouldn't be if someone had done as I asked."

"Damn women, always naggin'." Lincoln shuffled through the kitchen back to the bathroom.

"Watch your mouth."

"It's no problem," Matteo insisted before the siblings went for round two of their argument. "I've got my little helper here to assist." He winked at Norma.

The girl darted down the hall to the nook underneath the stairs that led to the upper level.

"Thank you. That drip was driving me crazy."

"You should've told me. I would've stopped by earlier to fix it."

"So I can be indebted to you more than I already am?"

"You're the only one keeping track of the things I do for you." He walked over and draped his hands on her shoulders. "As far as I'm concerned, you don't owe me anything."

"At least let me make you dinner." She pulled out of her tote bag the meatloaf sandwich he'd purchased at the diner. "You can save this for your lunch tomorrow."

"It's a deal."

She sealed their agreement with a peck to his cheek. The innocent gesture sent a shiver through him. He glanced over her head, lest he look down at her full lips and give in to the temptation to taste her.

His mind screamed that the right response would be to tell her he had forgotten a previous engagement, then walk out. But when it came to Bailey, Matteo could never find the strength to walk away.

"What do you need?" Norma pulled a chair from the table and placed on the seat the small red tin toolbox he'd left there years earlier, after he repaired a leak under her bathroom sink when Mr. Roberts was unable to tend to the chore.

"A wrench."

The girl rambled through the unorganized box. Her face lit up a second before she waved the tool in the air. "Miss Carroll let me help build the set for the school play."

"Your class is putting on a play?" Matteo opened the cabinet doors and ducked under the sink to shut off the water.

"Every class is doing one. Ours is in two weeks."

"Are you doing anything besides helping with the set?"

"Julia and I are narrators. We're gonna sit on the stage together and take turns introducing the characters."

Matteo's heart pounded at the mention of his daughter. He had not spoken to her in eighteen months. Unlike Bailey, his ex-wife upheld the family's decree. She would not have anything to do with him or allow their daughter to have contact with him.

He slid out from under the sink and sat on the floor. "Do you and Julia play together?"

"We're on the same jump rope team at recess," Norma replied, passing him the wrench.

"You're on a team?"

"Yes. We compete with the other girls to see who can jump the longest. I don't like jumping. I'd rather play tag, but only the boys are allowed to run around. So I turn the rope." Norma picked up a screwdriver and twirled it in her hands.

"Does Julia jump?"

"She's the best jumper in our grade. She can even jump longer than the third graders."

Matteo was impressed—but not surprised—by his daughter's accomplishment. At the age of five she would spend hours jumping rope in front of the house. His ex-wife used to complain the constant snap of the rope against the pavement interrupted her afternoon stories on the television. All he cared about was the fun the girl had.

"Do you do other things to—"

The refrigerator door slammed shut. Matteo glanced up at Bailey. Her arms were crossed over her chest, and her foot maintained a steady tap against the gray linoleum tile. He had crossed the line.

"Norma, did you finish your homework?" Bailey asked.

"I have to write my spelling," the girl replied.

"Go in the living room and write your words. I'll test you before you go to bed."

"But I was helping Mr. Matteo.".

"I'm sure he can finish up without you." Her eyes narrowed. "If not, he can leave it for Mr. Roberts."

Matteo had no desire to leave the job for someone

else. Not when all he had to look forward to at his place was an empty apartment.

"I can handle it," he said.

Norma dropped the screwdriver back into the toolbox. Her shoulders drooped as she dragged her feet out of the room.

Guilt weighed on Matteo. The girl should not have been punished for his indiscretion. Yet, thanks to the boundaries he'd crossed, there would be no more conversations with Norma that night.

Without a word, Matteo climbed to his feet to work on the sink's faucet, while Bailey added a package of ground beef to the pot on the stove.

****

Bailey waited until they finished eating and Norma was sitting cross-legged on the living room floor, watching *Leave It to Beaver*, before she chastised Matteo.

"I told you before I didn't want you interrogating Norma about Julia," Bailey said, sliding the bedroom doors closed.

Like his uncle had done for Georgia many years back, Matteo had provided Norma with an address that allowed her to enroll in a school outside her zone. Had she known he would grill her daughter for information about his, she would have reconsidered the gesture.

"I know," Matteo replied. "I'm sorry."

Bailey considered "I love you" and "I'm sorry" the two easiest phrases to utter without meaning them. Norma's father had professed his undying devotion to convince her to lie with him, then uttered his regret before taking off when she missed her monthly. Since then, she hesitated in believing the sincerity of anyone who uttered either of the phrases.

The remorse in Matteo's eyes made her not only want to forgive him but also to know, "Why?"

He rinsed the plate he had been scrubbing and placed it in the dish dryer before replying, "I miss her."

The confession tore at her heart. Julia had been everything to him. He had tried to make things work with his wife for the girl's sake. So when the woman packed his belongings and put him out of the house, the separation from his daughter nearly destroyed him.

Still, Bailey would not allow him to use her daughter. "Norma will not spy for you."

Matteo turned off the faucet, which he had fixed by the time supper was ready. "It won't happen again."

She tossed him a towel.

"I guess if I really cared about Julia, I would've thought about her before I started messing with that junk," Matteo said.

"Don't go there," Bailey said as she placed a bowl of leftovers in the refrigerator. "Perching on the pity pot isn't gonna do anyone any good."

Instead of following her advice, he continued. "Before the breakup, I would tell myself I was using for Julia's sake. I couldn't stand her mother, but at the same time I couldn't allow my daughter to be raised in a broken home, so I took a hit to help me deal with Eleanor. But the more I took, the more unhappy she became. In hindsight, I would've done everyone a favor if I had packed my bags and left."

"But you're not using anymore," Bailey said.

Matteo folded the towel and draped it over the bar hanging on the cabinet. "Like that's helped anything."

"It's gonna take time. You hurt a lot of people. You

can't expect them to forgive you overnight."

"Then how were you able to forgive me?"

She shrugged. Despite all his sins, Matteo had always been there for her. As much as she wanted to honor the family's wishes, she could not turn her back on him.

Chapter Five

The bedsprings squeaked, keeping time with Kyle's thrusts. Bailey arched her back. Her pelvis pushed up. Her thighs spread wider. And her groans filled the air as he pushed deeper inside her.

After the previous workout left them slumped across the bed at four in the morning, Bailey had hoped to sleep in. But when she woke to Kyle stroking her between her legs, she could not deny her body the satisfaction of finishing what he started.

Kyle's thrusts pushed her to the edge. Bailey held on tight to him as her body trembled, stars impaired her vision, and her breathing was reduced to gasps.

As she basked in the euphoria of her orgasm, Kyle pressed against her and shuddered with his release. Once the waves of pleasure began to subside, he dropped onto the mattress beside her. His face glowed with sweat and his chest rose and fell as he fought to catch his breath.

"How was it?"

The question was asked of her each time they were together. The first time, she had been honored, believing he cared whether she enjoyed herself. Since then, she realized he asked to reassure himself of his skills.

Though her reply would make him puff out his chest like a rooster showing off to a flock, she could not lie. "It was good." She reached for him, but he was already sitting up, offering her a view of his smooth, broad back.

Bailey's hand dropped to the mattress with a soft thud. Not for the first time, she was left wondering if that was it. They never held each other or talked. Hell, she was lucky if he said ten words to her before rolling over and going to sleep.

Thankfully, she had something better to do that day than to contemplate the emptiness she experienced whenever Kyle was finished with her.

"Where are you going?" he asked as she crawled off the bed.

"I'm taking Norma to the zoo."

"Enjoy yourselves." He stood up and walked towards the bathroom, showing no shame in his lack of attire.

While she had already made the plans with Matteo, Bailey was put off that Kyle had not asked if he could join them.

"We've never gone out together," she called after him as she picked her bra from the stack of clothes neatly folded on a chair at the foot of the bed.

"What do you mean?" Kyle poked his head into the room. "I took you out for dinner last night."

"I meant you, me, and Norma."

She took his nod as a positive sign. He quickly dashed her hopes when he mumbled, "We'll see," before he ducked back into the bathroom.

In the past, Bailey had been too preoccupied with her studies to worry about where they were headed. She did not have time to cultivate a relationship, and their weekly workouts had been good enough. But with her graduation behind her, she was ready to examine whether there was a future for all of them.

"What about next Saturday night?" she asked after

the toilet flushed.

"What about it?" His voice rose over the water splashing in the basin.

"How about the three of us go to the movies?"

Bailey cringed from the high-pitched squeak of the knob when he turned off the water. She was grateful for Matteo's diligence when it came to the repairs to her place. He tightened screws, adjusted hinges, and silenced the leaks, creaks, and shrieks from the pipes.

Another ten seconds passed before Kyle stepped back into the room and wrapped his arms around her. "I prefer Saturday nights to be about us." He pressed himself against her, emphasizing his point.

"Then how about Sunday?" Bailey asked.

Kyle leaned back and wrinkled his forehead. "What's bringing this on?"

"I wanted to talk about us."

"But I think I can find a better use of our time." He whispered the words into her neck, sending a shiver down her spine. "We can discuss this next week and enjoy the moment."

One large hand covered her breast and the other slipped between her folds. Her legs parted and she mentally chastised herself for being weak when it came to her body's desire.

When she crawled out of his bed a second time, Bailey showered and dressed. Not wanting to wait until he also washed and dressed, she declined his offer to drive her home. She gave him a long kiss, which she hoped would satisfy him until the following weekend, then skipped down a flight of steps to the first floor.

Outside, two girls dressed in frilly, starched yellow dresses, white ankle socks, and white patent leather shoes slowly walked past the building. White gloves covered their hands and small white handbags dangled from their arms. Their voices were just loud enough to reach each other's ears.

Bailey had given up trying to get Norma to look like a little lady. Her daughter had too much energy to sit quietly with other girls and talk, an activity that would keep her outfits pristine. No, she had to run, jump, and play as hard as the boys, which guaranteed specks of mud on her dress, loose strands of hair sticking out from her head, and encrusted blood marking the scrapes on her knees and elbows.

Ten minutes after leaving Kyle's apartment, Bailey walked across the street to her block. Her focus immediately locked in on Matteo, who sat on the steps leading to the upper apartments, smoking a cigarette. His gray polo shirt and beige slacks were a change from the t-shirts and denim pants he usually wore.

"When did you get here?" she asked when she reached the building.

"About nine. Thought we could get breakfast before we headed to the zoo."

Bailey glanced at her watch. "You've been waiting two hours?"

Though he'd arrived earlier than their agreed upon time, Bailey felt guilty to have kept him waiting while she enjoyed the company of another man.

Matteo shrugged his shoulders. "We'll have an early lunch."

"Norma isn't home yet from Sunday School."

No sooner had she finished the sentence when Norma raced around the corner with two girls who lived next door. As expected, one of her daughter's ribbons had come untied and hung half off her braid.

Norma stopped by Bailey's side as the other girls continued into their own basement apartment.

"Where's your purse?" Bailey asked, retying the ribbon.

She barely managed to suppress her laughter when Norma glanced wide-eyed at her bare arm.

Her babysitter stepped around the corner, swinging the scuffed white purse. Bailey took the bag and paid the teenager for her services.

"Come." Bailey motioned Norma to the apartment with one hand while waving at Matteo to follow.

He stood up and tossed the butt into the street, where two other cigarettes lay, before joining them.

Inside, Bailey snatched a pair of Lincoln's socks and an undershirt from the back of the armchair. "Have a seat," she said, gathering a dirty plate and an empty beer bottle from the coffee table. "We just need to change."

She closed the door dividing the living room and bedroom, then headed to the kitchen. After discarding the bottle in the bin in the corner and washing the plate, she tossed her brother's underclothes into a basket in the bathroom.

Bailey returned to the bedroom, where she changed from the dress she had worn the previous evening into a blue-and-white polka-dotted dress, and secured her hair at her nape with a blue ribbon. Once Norma had swapped her church clothes for a green checkered dress, she reopened the door.

Matteo pushed up from the sofa. A crooked smile slowly spread across his face as he took in her outfit.

"What?" Bailey asked.

"Last time I saw your hair pulled back, you were in

labor. You reminded me of a scared little girl."

"That's exactly what I was. What do I remind you of now?"

"A young woman taking a well-deserved day off." He wrapped a hand around hers. "You're not to worry about anything today. I'm taking care of everything."

Bailey pointed back at the kitchen. "At least, let me—"

"No."

"How about—"

"I won't hear of it."

"But—"

"Nope." Matteo shook his head.

Growing up, Bailey had been warned not to accept gifts from men, as they would always expect something in return…and usually that something would require her to lie back and spread her legs. But in the eight years he had been treating her, Matteo never asked for anything in return. And the one time they kissed, he had pulled back and insisted they could not be together.

"And no, I won't let you finish a sentence that doesn't start with, 'Okay,' " Matteo said.

Bailey huffed. "Okay, but how about—"

He peered over her shoulder. "Norma, are you ready?"

"Yes, Mr. Matteo." Her daughter shoved her Sunday dress into the wicker hamper next to the dresser. "Mommy, do I have to wear my sweater?"

Bailey held her hand out. "Give it to me and I'll carry it." Norma passed her the yellow sweater, which Georgia had crocheted, and skipped out of the house. "I guess we're ready."

Matteo waved her towards the door the girl left

77

open.

****

Bailey stood at the bottom of the steps, gaping at her surroundings. She reminded Matteo of a child visiting the zoo for the first time, and it suddenly hit him. "You've never been here before?"

Her gaze dropped as she shook her head. "I never had the time." There was regret in her voice when she made the confession. "Thanks to Norma's class trips, she didn't miss out."

Matteo hooked a forefinger under her chin and raised her head. "Hey, what's up, Shorty?"

Bailey sighed and her shoulders seemed to deflate. "Sometimes I think about everything Norma missed out on 'cause I was in school or had to work. I wanted her to know she had options in her future, but what did she have to give up now for that lesson?"

"Nothing." Matteo glanced at the girl who was reciting facts about the animals to an astounded zookeeper. Thanks to her mother, Norma had gained an appreciation for books that put her ahead of the other children in her class. "She doesn't act like she missed out on anything."

"Still, I'm glad I've graduated and was able to switch my schedule so I have more time to do things with her."

"Come on!" Norma waved at them.

Matteo's hand dropped to Bailey's shoulder as he led her to the entrance. Once they were inside, he allowed Norma to take the lead and direct them from one exhibit to the other, offering more facts about each animal.

He had made the same trip with his ex-wife and

daughter five years earlier, but it was not as intimate as this. Eleanor had kept no less than a yard between them and would not speak to him unless she was offering a curt one-word answer to a question.

Bailey, on the other hand, made certain there was no lull in the conversation. She encouraged him to contribute his thoughts and opinions on the topics they discussed. And when they did not see eye to eye, they simply agreed to disagree.

Thankfully, other than her preference for The Platters over The Flamingos, there were no other topics they could not come to a consensus on.

"What other sites haven't you visited?" he asked after they watched the seals.

"I've never been to Coney Island."

Her reply reminded him of how much she had to give up when she became pregnant. While their cousins were enjoying the rides at Steeplechase Park, indulging on hot dogs, popcorn, and cotton candy purchased from the stores along the boardwalk and enjoying the cool ocean breeze as they lay on the sand of the beach, she had been sitting in a classroom or retracing her steps from the dining room to the kitchen at the diner.

"How 'bout we take that trip next week?"

****

Though Kyle had yet to confirm their plans for the following Sunday, Bailey could not turn down a sure thing for a maybe. "I insist on packing a lunch."

He shook his head. "Part of the fun is the stomach ache you get from stuffing yourself with all the food along the boardwalk."

"That does *not* sound like fun."

"Trust me, it's memorable."

"You can't keep paying for everything," Bailey said. "I need to do something."

"You cooked dinner for me the other night."

Bailey crossed her arms over her chest and tapped her foot. The dinner had not counted. It was the least she could have done for him for fixing the leak in her faucet.

Matteo chuckled. "Okay, how 'bout we have a picnic the following week and you can make the sandwiches."

"Where?"

"We can head over to the museum, then have lunch in Mount Prospect Park."

Bailey was about to agree to the plan when Norma ran back to them.

"Mommy, I gotta go to the bathroom," Norma whispered, pointing to a brick building.

"Excuse us," she said, grateful for the rare demonstration of the girl's ability to lower her voice and not alert everyone to her business.

As Bailey waited in front of the last stall for Norma, a woman with a brunette bob and a mole on her chin cleared her throat.

"Excuse me," the woman whispered. "I noticed that man following you. If you tell security he's bothering you, they'll eject him."

Bailey bristled at the assumption regarding Matteo and her. Thanks to their different backgrounds, people made more out of their relationship than there was. In society's eyes, they could not simply be friends; either she was giving him some or he was harassing her.

The toilet flushed and the stall's door opened.

"Go wash your hands," Bailey said.

Norma glanced from her mother to the strange

woman before rushing to the sink near the door.

Once her daughter was on the other side of the room, Bailey replied to the woman, "I can assure you he's not bothering us. And, before you say anything else, the only dirty thing around here is the thought in your head."

Bailey marched over to the sink and turned off the water pouring over Norma's hands. She grabbed the girl's wrist and dragged her out of the bathroom.

"Mommy, my hands are still wet," Norma whined when they were three yards from the building.

Bailey released her daughter, opened her purse, and shoved a handkerchief into the girl's hand without breaking her stride. She continued until a hand wrapped around her forearm.

"Hey, Shorty, slow down." She stopped, and Matteo asked, "What's wrong?"

Bailey glared past him at the woman emerging from the bathroom. Their eyes locked and she saw the accusation formed by someone who did not know how many times he had been there for her.

She glanced back at Matteo and shook her head. Yes, he had made some mistakes…but none of them included placing a price tag on his friendship.

"What happened?" Matteo asked.

"Nothing." She tried to shake loose of his grip.

Instead of releasing her, he took both of her hands in his. "I'm not letting you go 'til you talk to me."

She recognized the stubborn glint in his eyes. The only thing that would force him to break his word would be her taking the woman's advice and alerting security.

Unwilling to pay him back for his kindness by making a scene, she stopped struggling. Matteo waited a heartbeat before retrieving a quarter from his pocket.

"Get us some popcorn." He tossed the coin to Norma.

The girl hesitated. Her brow wrinkled as her gaze moved from Matteo to her mother.

Not wanting her daughter to worry, Bailey forced herself to smile as she nodded her head. "It's okay, Busy Bee." Another second passed before Norma skipped away.

The smile faded as Matteo led Bailey to a nearby bench. She perched on the edge of the seat and he repeated, "What happened?"

"The woman in the bathroom accused you of bothering me," Bailey confessed.

He sat next to her and shrugged a shoulder. "And?"

"And I'm tired of people reading more into our relationship than there is."

"It was only one woman."

"And the people in my neighborhood." He raised an eyebrow, and she added, "I know people were whispering about me after I moved in. That is, until you and Nicholas bullied a few of the men."

With wide, innocent eyes, Matteo replied, "I didn't bully anyone."

"Then what would you call threatening them?" Bailey asked, crossing her arms over her chest.

"My fists just explained that it would be healthier for them to mind their own business and keep their opinions to themselves."

Bailey sighed. She finally understood the frustration Georgia felt when Nicholas insisted on solving problems with his fists.

Matteo took her hand with no concern over the looks tossed their way. "I intervened back then because you wanted to live on that block, and as long as you do, you should not be harassed. Your encounter with that woman lasted for as long as it took Norma to use the facilities. Don't let a five-second interaction ruin the rest of our day."

****

Determined to follow his own advice, Matteo rose and gently squeezed her hand. After a heartbeat, she stood and followed him away from the bench.

He held her hand as they strolled through the zoo, dispelling all assumptions he was harassing her and proving their relationship was deeper than a five-minute lay.

Though it was 1959, not 1859, tongues still wagged when women befriended someone of the opposite sex. Change the race of one of them and the rumors became tawdrier, as if only a colored woman of loose morals would associate with a white man.

Matteo knew walking away would be the easiest solution to their problems. Yet he could not give up the woman who, unlike his ex-wife, appreciated everything he did for her.

Hoping the ride would cheer them up, he led her to the carousel. He placed Norma on a brown horse and coaxed Bailey onto the gray animal parallel to the girl's. He then stood between the two females who meant as much to him as his daughter and were as equally off limits.

"Thank you for the afternoon," Bailey said as she stepped off the ride. Her features were brighter from laughing at his commentary on the race between her horse and Norma's.

"I hope you're not ready to call it a day." He passed

Norma her half-filled bag of popcorn.

"I thought we saw everything," Bailey replied.

"Not quite." He entwined her fingers with hers. "A day at the zoo is not complete without a stroll through the gardens." He pointed to the Brooklyn Botanical Gardens across the street.

Bailey agreed to the unscheduled trip and then to supper, with the day finally ending when Norma nodded off at the diner while eating lemon cake.

"I wish you'd put her down and let her walk," Bailey said as the bus pulled away from the curb near her apartment.

"It's no problem," Matteo insisted, carrying the sleeping girl. "She's worn out."

"I should think so. You had us walk all over the garden."

"I wanted to make sure you didn't miss anything."

"Why? Is it going somewhere?"

No, but there was no guarantee he would be with her the next time she went, and he'd wanted to watch her eyes brighten while she strolled through the Japanese Hill and Pond Garden and hear her take a deeper breath whenever she passed a thicket of flowers.

His contentment lasted until she pushed open her front door and Lincoln yelled, "Where the hell have you been?"

Her brother's tone was too harsh and too demanding for Matteo's comfort. Bailey, however, did not flinch as she walked past the half-dressed man as if he had not uttered a word.

"You can place her on the bed." She pointed to the bedroom.

Matteo laid Norma down, then stepped back so

Bailey could remove the girl's shoes.

"Well?" Lincoln asked.

"Wake this child and my whereabouts will be the least of your concerns." Bailey made the statement without glancing up from the shoe she was unbuckling.

Her brother slammed his palm against the wall before he marched back into the living room.

Growing up, Matteo had been taught not to get involved with other families' problems. But his conscience would not let him walk away from Bailey and Norma with Lincoln practically foaming at the mouth.

"Hey, man, what's up?" he asked.

"Been waitin' all afternoon for her to get home and make my dinner," Lincoln replied.

"Why couldn't you cook?" Bailey called after him.

"I was sleepin'. I gotta work tonight." Lincoln yanked on a white dress shirt.

"I told you I was going out. You should've picked something up on your way home."

"I figured you'd be back before now."

"Well, you figured wrong." Bailey stepped into the living room and closed the sliding door. "And, just so you'll know, I'm going out next week, too," she added before heading down the hall.

"What about me?" Lincoln asked.

"What about you?"

"I gotta eat."

Matteo followed the siblings to the kitchen. By the time he reached the room, Bailey was washing her hands. After a quick scrub, she yanked open the refrigerator door.

"When I let you move in, meals weren't part of our deal."

"Come on, woman," Lincoln whined. "Have a heart."

Bailey backed up with two packages wrapped in wax paper and a loaf of bread in one hand and a jar of mayonnaise in the other.

"You want a sandwich, Matteo?" she asked.

"No, thank you." If they hadn't eaten already, he would have lost his appetite at the display. His father never came home and ordered his wife to make dinner. He either waited patiently until she announced the food was ready, or he cooked his own meal. Matteo was therefore bothered not only by Lincoln's demand but by Bailey bowing down to him.

Bailey spread a glop of mayonnaise on each of two slices of bread, dropped two slices of bologna and a slice of cheese on top of one of those, then slapped the sandwich together.

"Here you go." She held out the sandwich.

Lincoln tucked in his shirt and grabbed the sandwich he could have made himself.

"Thanks, Sis." He kissed her check before rushing out of the room. "Don't wait up." A second later the front door slammed shut.

"Like I ever," Bailey mumbled, wrapping up the sandwich meat.

"Does he yell like that a lot?" Matteo asked.

"I don't know." Bailey shrugged a shoulder. "I don't pay him no mind most of the time."

He could not decide which response worried him more. A grown man's temper tantrum should not be rewarded. Yet what would be the consequences of her ignoring her brother?

Chapter Six

"You keep wiping at that window, you're gonna rub the glass away." Mrs. Murphy called up to Matteo.

Lost in his thoughts, he had not heard her return from the supermarket, despite the squeaking wheels on her shopping cart. He dropped the hand holding the rag and stared through the half-open pane at the woman. In the time it had taken her to go to the store and return with a wagon full of groceries, all he'd accomplished was to create streaks that distorted his view.

"What's wrong?" Mrs. Murphy brow wrinkled with concern.

"Rough night." Matteo sighed, wishing the dreams had disappeared when he climbed out of bed. To his dismay, the rising sun had not erased the images that plagued him since he left Bailey's apartment the previous evening.

"Something you ate?" she asked.

"It was more like something someone else ate."

Lincoln's overreaction to dinner had awakened memories he'd thought buried. The distorted features he had seen in the mirror as he screamed at his wife, the thud from his fist slamming into the wall and, most importantly, the heartbreaking cries of his daughter had been replaying in his mind.

Mrs. Murphy tilted her head forward and glanced over the top of her glasses at Matteo. He realized he had not made any sense.

"I'm worried about a friend," he clarified as he mentally compared his reaction to Eleanor making steak instead of chicken for dinner to Lincoln's tantrum at Bailey not fixing dinner. As much as he wanted to deny it, he had to consider the possibility the other man was using drugs.

"Come have some cake," Mrs. Murphy said.

While his fondness for sweets was the only addiction he had not kicked, he was not in a sociable mood. He was preparing to decline the offer when she scowled at him. Refusing was not an option.

"I'll be right out to get your cart," Matteo replied, tossing the rag into his toolbox.

In the thirty seconds it had taken him to make it to the front door, Mrs. Murphy had pulled the shopping cart up the stoop.

"I said I'd get that." Matteo took the wagon from her. "You gonna have people thinking I'm not a gentleman."

"People always gonna find something to talk about." She pssted. "You pay these busybodies around here no mind. I know how much you help everyone in this building and that's all that matters." She patted his arm before releasing her load.

Matteo carried the cart to the second floor. The aroma of the hearty stew simmering on the back burner of the stove greeted them when Mrs. Murphy opened her door. The smell conjured up the memories of his parents' house and made him nostalgic for the days before he let everything but the brain between his ears control him.

In the kitchen, Mrs. Murphy waved at the double-basin porcelain sink. "You can clean up there."

Matteo scrubbed the dust from his hands while she retrieved plates from the cabinet over the stove and two forks from the drawer under the counter.

She removed the glass top from the silver tray sitting in the middle of her table. The knife slid through the thick layer of white frosting into the moist chocolate cake. She tipped the large slice onto the plate, then set it on the blue vinyl tablecloth.

Matteo dried his hands on a paper towel he ripped from the roll hanging on the wall over the sink. Sliding into a green chair at the table, he accepted a fork from the woman—and groaned with contentment as he savored the sweet, moist dessert.

"Anyone inquired about the apartment?" Mrs. Murphy asked about the recently vacated space he had been renovating.

"Mrs. Cronetti," Matteo replied.

The timing had been perfect for the recently widowed woman, whose only child had married and moved cross-country two years earlier.

"Yes, that would be perfect for her." Mrs. Murphy cut another slice of cake, then tossed the knife into the sink. "I remember feeling so lost in my two-bedroom apartment after my husband passed. It was too much for one person. Of course, if I had known I'd end up with Liam, I'd have stayed put."

Matteo glanced out of the kitchen and down the small hall to the living room they passed through when they entered the apartment. The space was not the most ideal for the older woman and her grandson.

He jerked his head to the left, in the direction of the soon-to-be-vacated apartment. "You should move into Mrs. Cronetti's apartment."

Mrs. Murphy shook her head as she chewed the bite she had placed in her mouth. "I'm not moving again," she said after she swallowed. "It'll only be a matter of time before Liam moves out and I'll be stuck with another two-bedroom place. No, we've managed all these years, so what's a couple more." She pointed her fork at the wall. "A young couple, expanding their family, would have more use for the apartment."

Or it would be the ideal apartment for a young mother with a growing daughter who deserved to have her own room, where she could play with her toys and enjoy sleepovers. And, with him keeping an eye on them, neither would have to deal with an irrational squatter who tossed crap all over the living room and made demands he was perfectly capable of accomplishing for himself.

Bailey, however, would not give up her apartment. The seventy-dollar monthly rent was a steal, and she would never believe him if he told her she could get the two bedrooms for the same she was already paying.

A tap on the hand startled Matteo. He raised his gaze from the cake he had picked apart while lost in his own head.

"Unburden your mind," Mrs. Murphy said.

"I'm worried about a friend." He pushed his plate aside and sat back.

"You mentioned that before. Why are you concerned? Did someone hurt her?"

He was not going to guess how she knew the person he was worried about was a female. Instead, he addressed the question with, "Not yet."

"But something happened for you to suspect she could be hurt?"

He nodded.

"As a friend, you can't keep your suspicions to yourself."

"I know, but—"

"It's someone close to her?" Mrs. Murphy asked.

"Yes, ma'am."

"It doesn't change anything…well, except for the possibility of you losing her friendship once you reveal your suspicions."

Matteo was more concerned about what Bailey would do about Lincoln. Out of the ten siblings she had, her brother was the only immediate family member… aside from Norma…who associated with her. There was a chance the others would reach out to her after they were grown and on their own. But until then, would she be willing to confront Lincoln or would she turn a blind eye to the man's faults and the possible dangers of sheltering him?

****

Despite sitting through three stories, eighteen sets of eyes begged Bailey for "one more." Feeling her resolve crumble, she glanced towards the librarian pushing the cartload of books down a row of shelves.

Having been at the facility since ten that morning, Clara Ramos had no problem denying their requests thirty minutes before closing time. "That's enough stories for today. Miss Collins will read more next week."

Bailey raised her voice to be heard over the grumbles. "Get your things and line up to check out your books."

The children uncrossed their legs and jumped up from the floor, where they had sat as she read. Ignoring the multitude of signs posted around the room, reminding visitors to keep the noise down, they ran to the shelves to grab coveted books before they were claimed by others.

"They can't get enough of you," Clara said, ignoring the rambunctious behavior.

The feeling was mutual. Bailey enjoyed reading to the children as much as they seemed to enjoy listening.

What had started as a desire to introduce Norma to books had turned into a weekly storytime after their second trip to the library. As she had read to her daughter, another child inched towards them until he was sitting by her side. The following week, two other children joined the group. By the end of the month, children were passing her books they wanted her to read.

Bailey picked up the books she had stacked on the floor next to her foot when she finished with them.

"I'll take those," Clara said as Bailey stood up from the wooden chair she had used while she read. "I'm sure the children could use some help picking out books."

The time she had spent around the children, some of them for all of the six years she had been patronizing the library, had given her a sense of the reading levels for many of them and allowed her to recommend books based on what she read, or the reports made by Norma and the other avid young readers.

Once the children were waiting to check out their books, Bailey wandered to the shelves that housed her favorite collection. Her heart sank as she stared at the large gap between two titles. It was not unusual for one book to be missing, but all three?

A quick glimpse at her watch confirmed there was not enough time for her to search for something else.

Resigning herself to the fact she would be going without reading material for a week, Bailey returned to the front.

"Couldn't find anything?" Clara closed the ink pad she used to stamp the due date on the borrowing cards.

"Everything's checked out," Bailey replied.

"I think I have something you may enjoy." The woman retrieved a brightly wrapped package from underneath her desk.

Bailey became aware of the sudden hush that echoed through the library. Eighteen children gathered around the checkout desk, beaming like they were ready to explode from a secret.

Clara counted to three and the deafening cries of, "Congratulations," filled the room.

Bailey blinked back the tears and swallowed the lump lodged in her throat.

"You need a minute to compose yourself?" Clara asked.

She shook her head. "I'll be fine," she said, wiping away the tear sliding down her cheek.

"Norma told us a month ago you were graduating." She nudged the package towards Bailey. "We took up a collection to get you this."

Bailey accepted the package and gently peeled the paper back. She smiled at the new copies of her favorite Langston Hughes titles.

"We decided to buy you copies so others can have a chance to read them."

She rolled her eyes. She could not help it if the antics of Hughes' protagonist, Jesse B. Simple, amused her.

"Thank you. I'll always cherish this."

Bailey accepted hugs from the children, her daughter included, before the chatter moved to the street and all one could hear was the rustle of turning pages and the scratches from pencils moving across notebook paper.

"Hope you're not too upset with Norma for telling your business." Clara reached across the desk for the wooden tray used to store the cards pulled from the back of the books that were checked out. "She's proud of her mother."

Bailey shook her head. "I learned long ago never to tell a child something you didn't want others to know."

"Good advice." The librarian chuckled. "You know you're an inspiration, not only to the children, but to some of the adults around here."

Bailey's brow furrowed. She did not think she'd done anything spectacular.

"Not too many women go to college, and even fewer colored women attend. But you're an unwed colored mother. After hearing about your achievement, a few mothers talked about taking classes at the community college."

Bailey felt a sense of pride knowing she had a positive influence on some of the parents.

"What are you planning to do now?"

"Look for a job." Bailey offered her standard reply despite Nicholas's job offer.

"Have you ever considered working in the library?" Clara asked.

Bailey shook her head.

"You should. You love books, you work well with the children, and you're always coming up with ideas that will benefit the patrons."

Suggesting a mentoring program that would pair high school students with the younger children didn't seem special. She had simply figured the older children would be inspired to stay in school if they had someone looking up to them and the younger students would benefit from having the older role models.

"Miss North is retiring at the end of the summer." Clara pointed to the white-haired colored woman across the room. "You would need to go back for a degree in library science, but while you're working towards that, you could start off as a clerk."

Bailey's gaze moved across the shelves behind them. She was certain there was more to being a librarian than reading to the children, yet it was an incentive to consider the position. Not only would she be able to expand reading time to more than one day a week, something the children had been begging her to do for years, but she could divide the times for different reading levels.

She would need to consider the extra years of schooling. The time she had taken from Norma to get her bachelor's degree was justified when she had been trying to be a role model for the girl. Having achieved her goal, she could not put her daughter through two more years of night and weekend classes.

"Think about it," Clara said.

After promising she would consider her options, Bailey headed outside and announced to Norma it was time to go home.

Hugging the second and third books in the Nancy Drew series to her chest, Norma skipped down the street and offered an account of her day. Bailey had as much interest in Julia's new dress, Diane's new shoes, and the argument the two girls engaged in over whose looked better as she did in watching a faucet drip. Yet she hung onto every word—well, maybe every other word—reminding herself the girl would not be young forever. Her daughter would eventually grow up, move out, and take the chatter with her.

The Chantels were serenading the neighbors when Bailey turned onto her block. Mortified the noise was coming from her apartment, she hastened her steps to the building.

Her ears pounded from the high volume of the radio, and her eyes watered from the stench of burnt eggs and bacon. She stepped over a pair of pants lying on the floor, reached for the radio, and encountered a nub where the volume dial was supposed to be. Feeling her patience running thin, she yanked the plug from the wall.

"What the f—?" Lincoln called from the kitchen.

"Watch your language." Bailey yelled over the ringing in her ears.

Her brother strolled into the living room, wearing a stained undershirt and boxers. "Why'd you go turn off my music?"

"Why was it so loud?"

"I wanted to hear it in the kitchen."

"I could hear it down the block." She grabbed the slacks by her foot and tossed them at him. "Put some clothes on. Norma don't need to see all your business."

He held his hands out and glanced down. "What? I'm covered."

"Don't matter. Get dressed," she ordered as she stepped around him and headed to the kitchen.

Bailey stopped in the threshold and gaped at the pair of legs peeping out of the cabinet under the sink.

"What are you doing under there?" she asked.

"I'm looking for clues," Norma replied, her voice

muffled by the enclosure.

"What clues?"

"For the mystery. I'm gonna be like Nancy Drew and solve mysteries and go on adventures."

Bailey chuckled. "While you're under there, please pass me the shortening."

"Hey, Sis, lend me a nickel," Lincoln said.

She spun around and rolled her eyes as her brother strolled into the kitchen, buttoning his pants. "You got some nerve asking me for money. You still owe me rent, which, by the way, is due today."

"I'm a little short. I had to take my woman out. You know I'm good for it."

"When?"

"Don't sweat it. I'll give you the money this weekend."

Ignoring the little voice in her head telling her, "No," Bailey fished her change purse from the side pocket on her dress and pulled out a five-dollar bill.

"I want it back Sunday morning," she said.

"You'll get it." He snatched the money from between her fingers with one hand and mussed her hair with the other. "Thanks."

Bailey bit back the instinct to say, "No problem," because it *was* a problem. Her brother was being irresponsible, and instead of demanding he do better, she was enabling his behavior.

Chapter Seven

Bailey snorted when The Platters' "Twilight Time" faded and Vaughn Monroe began singing "What a Difference a Day Makes"—no truer words had been spoken. In twenty-four little hours, Norma went from searching the cabinets and closets for more clues to being tucked under the covers looking miserable.

Bailey shook her head as she traced the mercury in the thermometer to one hundred. "You're not going to be much of a Busy Bee for several days," she announced.

"Am I gonna miss the class play?" Norma's scratchy voice reminded her of a tire rolling over gravel.

Though it was Saturday evening, Bailey reckoned Norma would be fine by Wednesday. "If you stay in bed and rest, I think you'll be better by then. I'll bring you a cup of tea."

"Okay," Norma replied, curling up underneath the blanket. Bailey tucked a colored rag doll next to her before rising from the bed. A knock on the front door paused her trip to the kitchen.

Deciding she wanted to get the water on the stove, she called out, "Just a minute."

She filled a small pot from the faucet and placed it on the back burner before rushing to confront the visitor trying to pound a hole through the door.

"Is that racket necessary?" she asked, snatching open the door.

"It is when you take so long to answer," Kyle replied, stepping into the apartment. "You ready?"

Both eyebrows shot up. She had left a message at the funeral parlor, saying she would have to cancel. It was right after she called the diner to tell them she would not be in that morning and before she phoned Matteo to cancel their outing to Coney Island.

"Didn't you get my message? Norma's sick."

"What does that have to do with us?" Kyle asked.

Bailey flinched. Had she heard him correctly?

"Lincoln can stay with her. It's not like he has a job," the man added.

Taken back by the suggestion that she leave her sick daughter to go out with him, it took a second before his statement completely sank in. "What do you mean Lincoln's not working?"

"He hasn't had a job in three months."

That was impossible. Her brother left every evening at six and did not return until the following morning. If he was not in Harlem tending bar, then what was he doing for twelve hours? And where was he getting the money to pay his portion of the rent?

Realizing she would not get the answers to her questions until the next morning, she focused on the more important matter.

"It doesn't matter," Bailey said. "I'm not leaving my baby."

"This your way of getting back at me 'cause I didn't want her tagging along on our date?" Kyle asked.

The man was showing her a new side of himself, and while she did not particularly like it, she was grateful it was coming out sooner rather than later.

Bailey pointed a forefinger at her chest. "I'm

Norma's mother and I will not leave her when she's sick."

"And you're my woman." Kyle held his hands out from his side. "At least, so I thought," he added, dropping his arms.

"Yes, but Norma comes first—"

"Second and third."

Bailey crossed her arms over her chest. "What does that mean?"

"It means you always use her as an excuse not to go out. You can't hang out on a weeknight 'cause she has school. Come the weekend, you bail on me 'cause she has the sniffles."

"Would you really want to go out with a woman who's not there for her baby?"

"I want you to find time for me like you do that white man who's always hanging around."

Bailey's mouth dropped open. Someone was in her business—again.

"I know about that man coming here every night and not leaving 'til morning."

Of course, the busybodies would exaggerate the frequency and length of the visits.

Yes, Matteo visited often, but he was not over every day. And, while he had slept on her sofa the night his wife kicked him out, he had not stayed over anytime during the two years she had been with Kyle.

"Matteo's an old friend. He rides home with me and offers to fix things around the apartment."

"And exactly what is he fixing?"

Since green was her least favorite color, she said, "I'm going to pretend I didn't hear that." Norma's cough told Bailey it was past time she ended the conversation.

She placed her hand on his cheek. "We can talk about this another time."

"Yeah, whatever." Kyle shoved his hands in his pockets and marched up the steps to the yard.

Bailey swore she felt steam rising from her head. He had some nerve, expecting her to place his needs before her daughter's. Yeah, he showed his true colors.

Bailey closed the door and returned to the kitchen to brew the tea. Determined to be present for her baby both physically and mentally, she pushed her conversation with Kyle to the back of her mind.

Norma sat up when she walked back into the bedroom with a ceramic pink elephant mug. Her scrunched face relayed her feelings for the bitter brew.

Despite her distaste for the drink, Norma drank the tea, then held up the cup. Bailey placed the mug on the end table and climbed onto the bed. The girl leaned against her side as she reached for a copy of *The Borrowers*.

"I'm sorry I ruined your evening, Mommy," Norma said.

"What do you mean, Busy Bee?" Bailey asked.

"Mr. Winters said I'm the reason you don't go out."

Guilt slammed into Bailey like a fist to her gut, knocking the wind from her. Why hadn't she stepped outside and closed the door? Better for her neighbors to hear the disagreement and add more fuel to the gossip mill than for Norma to think she was the cause of any strife in her life.

Bailey pulled Norma onto her lap and held her tight. "Mr. Winters was wrong. And don't you ever let anyone make you believe you're a problem. In fact, you're my little inspiration."

Norma's wide brown eyes stared up at her. "What do you mean?"

"You were the reason I got the courage to stand on my own two feet. You're the reason I went back to school, and when things seemed impossible, it was the thought of you that kept me going. You're also the reason I get up each morning and go to work. And you're the reason I can't wait to get home every evening." She placed a kiss on the girl's warm forehead. "I know it's hard for you to understand, but one day…hopefully after you're married…you will."

"How come you didn't marry my father, like Julia's mother?" Norma asked.

Bailey's brow furrowed. "What are you talking about?"

"Julia told me her parents married 'cause her mother was pregnant with her."

As far as Bailey was concerned, Julia's mother talked too much. However, she knew better than to utter her opinion. The comment would get back to the other woman and spread through the entire school.

When Bailey first arrived in New York, shame had caused her to stay indoors and take care of her uncle's apartment when she wasn't working. Georgia had thought it would be fun for her to get out and insisted she attend Matteo's wedding with her. As the bride and groom exchanged vows, she had to force back the tears while she wondered why Norma's father had bailed on her instead of taking care of his responsibilities.

Hell, upon his insistence, she had proven her commitment to him by allowing him under her skirt. Yet when the time came for him to show how much he cared, he was nowhere to be found.

After watching Matteo and his wife, Bailey decided being abandoned by Norma's father had been the best thing for her.

Matteo had never been able to hide how miserable he was in his marriage. Bailey could not imagine living with someone who was only there for appearances. Besides, had she married, she probably would not have gone back to school and been an example for Norma.

Bailey squeezed her tight. "Trust me, everything has worked out the way it should."

****

Liam shuffled into the apartment and slumped in the chair in the center of the room. His foot jostled the card table and upset the bottle of root beer.

Thankfully, Matteo had polished off all but a swallow of the soda. He dropped the roller he had been using to repaint the pale green wall white and reached for the rag draped over the back of the chair.

"No date tonight?" Matteo asked, mopping up the brown drops. If only fixing the mess he'd made of his life were as easy.

"'Course I do." Liam draped his right arm around the air next to him. "Ain't she a beaut?"

"You're lucky I like you. Smart mouth like yours would've got popped in my house, growing up."

Liam dropped his arm to his side and rolled his eyes. His was not the most ideal response, but at least he did not suck his teeth and mutter, "Whatever."

"Mind if I hang out here?" Liam asked.

Matteo tossed the rag onto the table, pulled a paint brush from the tin box, and held it out to the youngster. If the kid was going to hang around, he might as well work.

Liam took the brush and pushed up from his chair. Though he had never gotten away with lounging around while Matteo worked, he made a show of rolling his eyes and sucking his teeth.

"How come you never go out?" he asked, dipping the brush in the pan of paint. "You're not into chicks?"

Matteo snorted. It would have been easier if he didn't like women instead of being attracted to the one he could not have.

"Why aren't *you* out instead of painting apartments on a Saturday night?" he asked, picking up the roller.

"Umm…well…you know…" The boy stumbled over his words while shifting from one foot to the other.

Matteo nodded. "What's her name?"

Liam face reddened. "Carmen." His gaze dropped to the floor.

"And why are you here instead of with her?"

Liam shrugged his shoulders. The nonverbal reply and the avoidance of eye contact did not sit well with Matteo.

"Spill it." The tone used to issue the command reminded him of his father. The older man could elicit a full confession from his sons with just the two words and a deep, stern voice.

"She's not exactly talking to me."

Knowing there was no such thing as someone "not exactly talking" to someone else, he asked, "What did you do?"

"Nothing." The reply was too quick for Matteo's liking. He dropped the roller and crossed his arms over his chest until the boy admitted, "The guys decided to play T-and-A with her."

Matteo bristled at the game in which boys try to cop

a feel as a woman walked by them. The males got a point if they touched her breast or rear and three if they succeeded in groping both before she got away. The girl was left feeling dirty, humiliated, and confused, according to Celeste, who had been forced to walk a gauntlet of horny boys one afternoon.

The memory of a fourteen-year-old Celeste begging the boys to leave her alone flashed in his mind. Instead of letting her pass, they'd laughed in her face.

The laughter stopped when Matteo and Nicholas showed up and made sure the boys would be unable to touch their own rears much less anyone else's for a least a month.

"And you decided to join them?" Matteo asked.

"No, I didn't do anything," Liam insisted.

Red clouded Matteo's vision. It was bad enough the girl was assaulted, but the boy stood by and did nothing.

Was this what his little girl had to look forward to? Providing entertainment for the bored and horny? And what would happen if she spoke out against the unwanted attention?

When the haze faded, Liam was pinned against the wall. Matteo's knuckles ached from his grip on the boy's shirt and the back of his hands stung from the jagged nails clawing the skin.

The fear in the boy's eyes did not stir any sympathy in Matteo. "Women are to be respected." His voice deepened as he enunciated each word.

"It's not a big deal." Liam struggled to balance himself on the tips of his toes. "They didn't mean anything by it."

"What if that was your grandmother?" Matteo pulled the boy forward and bellowed in his face, "Would it still be no big deal?"

Trembling, the boy whipped his head from side to side.

"Did she ask to be touched?" Matteo asked.

"N…n…n…no," Liam stuttered.

"Was she laughing?"

Liam's Adam's apple bobbed up and down. "No."

"Then it was a big deal."

Matteo released the boy and stepped back before he gave in to the temptation to slam his fist into the youngster's face. Taking advantage of his freedom, Liam beat a hasty retreat from the room. Seconds later, the apartment door slammed against the freshly painted wall.

"*Merda!*" Matteo's expletive vibrated off the walls. Some role model he was. Mrs. Murphy had trusted him to be an example to her grandson. But in eighteen months he had not accomplished anything.

Chapter Eight

Bailey muttered a curse as she stared at the bottle of syrup she retrieved from the cabinet. There was barely enough to cover half a silver-dollar pancake. Lincoln had warned her they were running low and had asked her to pick up another bottle when she went to the market on Saturday, yet, in a hurry to return home, she had forgotten it, along with the jam Norma preferred.

She dropped the bottle in the garbage and walked into the bedroom.

"I have to run to the store," she said, slipping her feet into her canvas shoes. "Stay in bed."

"Yes, Mommy," Norma muttered without glancing up from the book she'd grabbed the second her eyes popped open.

Bailey snatched a dollar from her purse and hurried outside. She made it as far as the gate, and then Kyle stepped out of the building across the street, wearing the same suit he had on the previous evening. Her blonde neighbor stood in the doorway wearing a short cream-colored satin robe and—Bailey was willing to bet the dollar balled up in her fist—nothing else underneath.

All noise on the block seemed to cease. Not a bird chirped, nor did a horn bleep nor a leaf rustle in the wind. Everyone seemed to hold their breaths as they glanced from one woman to the other.

Kyle shifted from one foot to the other. His mouth

opened and closed as if he was going to say something but changed his mind. Behind him, his lady of the evening smirked, her eyes dancing in victory.

Before going to bed the previous evening, Bailey had decided to talk to Kyle—give him a chance to understand her priorities. The past two years had been fun, and she did not want to throw it all away. Yet seeing him walk out of that woman's house changed everything.

Bailey pushed back her shoulders and marched across the street with her head held high. With each step she took, her nemesis' bravado faded until a frown replaced the grin and she was visibly shaking.

She stopped two steps below the couple and snatched the gold chain from her own neck. "It appears you earned this more than I did." She tossed the necklace at the other woman's feet, turned, and headed back down.

"Babe, wait up." Kyle rushed past her and stood on the bottom step. "It's not what you think. I only banged that piece of tail 'cause you weren't givin' me any last night."

"What?" The other woman called him a name that was not far from the truth since Bailey was a mother and Kyle had fornicated with her the previous weekend.

Despite the woman's profanity-laced grumble, Kyle did not shift his focus from Bailey. His eyes silently begged her to listen to his excuse and forgive his indiscretion.

Bailey shook her head. "Now you're free to be with her every night." She stepped around him and continued back across the street.

Lincoln stood in front of the building, smiling. "I'm proud of you, Sis," he said, following her into the apartment. "You handled that with class."

"It was still humiliating." She tightened her fist and remembered the dollar bill and her errand. "Damn, I need to go to the store for syrup and jam."

"No, you don't." Lincoln held out a bag.

Bailey took the package. Inside were the items she had intended to purchase, along with a slab of bacon.

"How'd you pay for these?"

"With money." Lincoln slipped off his jacket and dropped it on the chair. "Here you go." He held out several bills.

Bailey counted eight fives, which covered his portion of the rent and the nickel he owed her.

"According to the grapevine, you haven't had a job in three months," she said, slipping the money into the front pocket of her dress.

He shrugged his shoulders. "Things didn't work out."

"Then where are you getting the money to pay for everything?"

"I'm payin' my share. What does it matter where I get my money?"

"It *does* matter."

"Why you raggin' on me? I don't hear you gettin' all righteous with Matteo."

Bailey conceded. She never questioned Matteo about the work he did for his family. She simply accepted his friendship and prayed neither the law nor another family forced him to retire before he was ready.

"I know what I'm doing." Lincoln gripped her arms. "Trust me."

Knowing he was going to do what he wanted whether she agreed with him or not, Bailey huffed,

"Fine." She added a special prayer he did not get in over his head with whatever scheme he was involved in.

"Good." He mushed her hair. "Now, what do you say about feeding me before I go to sleep?"

She pulled away from him. "For that, I should make you cook your own food," she said even as she headed towards the kitchen to prepare their meal.

****

"You missed dinner," Mrs. Murphy announced, stepping into the room as Matteo stirred the peach paint Mrs. Cronetti had picked out for the bathroom.

"I needed to get this done." He mumbled the reply he'd prepared in the event the woman sought him out for skipping the meal.

"It's not nice to bullshit an old woman."

Matteo jerked back at the uncharacteristic language and dropped the brush into the paint can.

Mrs. Murphy leaned against the side of the bathtub and continued as if she had not used language he had always been warned never to utter around ladies. "When Liam's father was ten, him and his friends thought it would be fun to shake their willies at the girls. My husband caught 'em, and that boy couldn't sit for a week afterward."

Her story was not unfamiliar. In his family, depending on the severity of the transgression, a punishment could be as light as a pop upside the back of the head to a wallop that tenderized a seat for a day or two.

"The punishment was not easy on any of us, but it went a long way in him growing up to be a man I was proud of, and I know he would not have spared disciplining Liam." She leaned forward and laid a hand on his arm. "Don't be ashamed of having raised your voice to Liam 'cause he stepped out of line."

Matteo shook his head. He was not sorry he yelled at the boy. He regretted it had been necessary. "If I had been a better role model…"

The spark of understanding lit up her eyes. "Nonsense." She straightened and placed her hands on her hips, similar to the stance his grandmother would take before delivering a lecture.

Expecting the conversation was going to last several more minutes, he lowered himself to the floor, stretched one leg out in front him, and hugged the other to his chest.

"It's natural to wonder where you went wrong when your child does something contrary to what you taught 'im. But remember even the best kid strays. And when they do, it's not a reflection on you."

Thinking back to his family, Matteo recognized the truth behind her words. His father had warned him about drugs and their ability to cloud a person's judgment. To run a successful business, one stayed clear of the mind-altering chemicals and watched the alcohol consumption.

Despite the numerous lectures, he got shit-faced and lay with a girl without using a glove. He then turned to something stronger to cope with the consequences of that night.

"Instead of beating yourself up, treat an error in judgment as a learning opportunity. What can you do to help him in the future?"

****

"You need any help?" Liam slouched against the doorjamb about an hour after his grandmother returned to her apartment. He tried to play it cool, yet Matteo suspected the boy's hands would have been shaking had they not been shoved in the front pockets of his jeans.

Offering the boy the second chance his family would not give him, Matteo pointed to the broom leaning in the opposite corner, next to the kitchen sink.

Liam pushed away from the wall and shuffled across the dusty floor. He grasped the broom handle, shook his head, and sighed.

"I'm sorry for…well…you know…" He stumbled over the words as he stared into the corner.

Matteo turned away from the curtain rod he had been installing. "I can't forgive you."

The boy spun around. His downcast gaze spoke of his disappointment. "You can't?"

"It wasn't my tit that was touched," Matteo elaborated.

Liam nodded his head. "I guess I should apologize to her."

"Yes." Matteo resumed to the job he hoped to complete before he went to bed so Mrs. Cronetti could move in the next day. "Though I'd work on that apology, if I were you."

"What was wrong with it?"

"You first need to look the recipient of the apology in the eye."

"Um…okay…"

"And you don't beat around the bush like a punk. Man up and spit it out." Matteo climbed down from the ladder and crossed his arms over his chest.

"Fine." Liam dragged the broom in a circle over the floor.

"And you better make sure you damn well mean it.

Nothing worse than someone apologizing and then turning around and doing the same shit again."

"I mean it."

"Why'd you do it?"

Liam shrugged his shoulders.

The passive reply angered Matteo. His hand balled into a fist as he imagined the boy having the same reaction while the girl was looking for someone to save her.

Determined to be the role model Mrs. Murphy wanted for her grandson, Matteo took a second to rein in his emotions. He took a deep breath, then forced his voice to remain calm as he repeated, "Why'd you do it?" The inflection in his tone conveyed his desire for a verbal answer.

Liam shifted from one foot to the other before he finally admitted, "The guys thought it'd be fun."

"You always go along with the guys?"

"They're my friends…you know how it is."

Unfortunately, Matteo knew exactly how it was. "They're your friends 'til the shit blows up." And in some cases they were the ones responsible for the mess.

Gianni Acardis had been Nicholas's friend for twenty years, yet after eloping with Celeste, he broke the Santiano code and beat her, a sin Matteo would have foreseen had he not been under the influence of the drugs Gianni had introduced him to years earlier.

Matteo realized he was ultimately responsible for his own actions. He had been the one to go out in search of a good time instead of trying to make things work with his wife. It had been his choice to tag along with Gianni to the basement apartment in a rundown building. And he had chosen to stick the rolled-up bill to his nose instead of walking away.

Believing the boy could learn from his mistakes, Matteo pointed to the chair he had been moving from room to room as he worked.

Liam dropped the broom and sat. Matteo passed the young man a cola before relaying the events that led to his being an outcast with his family.

Chapter Nine

After six years of reading to children, who squirmed and blurted out comments that were amusing in their heads but not to the ears of the adults, Bailey was not easily distracted when she read. However, the unusual amount of chatter from the checkout desk fueled her curiosity. As she turned to the next page in *Popo and Fifina*, she glanced over the children's heads at Matteo.

He leaned against the first row of shelves, his gaze locked on her. To the casual observer, he appeared entranced by the story. Bailey knew better. The man was dreaming up devilment as he was apt to do whenever he visited the library.

While she was grateful for his ability to spark Norma's curiosity, she could have done without the volcano that had her wiping up "lava" from the table and floor and the ants that escaped the farm he bought for her.

A young woman who had been employed at the library for two weeks approached him and whispered in his ear. The corner of his lips rose to a smirk. He leaned in and, without taking his eyes off Bailey, he offered his reply just as quietly.

The woman stepped back. Her jaw went slack, and her gaze darted around the room. As she seemed to search her mind for the appropriate action, Carla pushed a cart towards the couple and passed it off to the woman.

The young woman walked off with the books, glancing from Matteo to Bailey. With her hands on her hips, Carla scolded the man, who tried…and failed…to look innocent of all sins.

Rolling her eyes, Bailey went back to the book, focusing on the text until the last page. As soon as she closed the book, the children begged for another story. Before she could go through the routine of checking with those in charge, Carla announced it was time to pick out books to take home.

"You've got company." Carla tilted her head at Matteo as the children dispersed.

"I saw," Bailey said.

"When are you two going to stop playing games and get serious?"

Bailey showed no reaction to Carla's bluntness, a far cry from the gasp that had her coughing for a minute the first time the woman brought up the subject.

Carla was sure Matteo's intentions towards Bailey went beyond friendship, and no arguments—including his previous marital status and his family disowning him—could convince her otherwise. Of course, it did not help when Bailey had become flustered and tripped over her words at that first mention.

The glint in Carla's eyes dared her to speak without hemming and hawing. Not up for the challenge she knew she would fail, Bailey walked off to assist the children.

"Have you thought about what we discussed last week?" Carla asked when all the children had skipped out of the building with their latest finds tucked under their arms a half hour later.

"I'm considering it."

Bailey had given Nicholas the same reply when he

stopped by the previous afternoon to ask her to join the family for Sunday dinner. Truthfully, since getting the offers, she had spent all her free time weighing the pros and cons of each and was no closer to deciding.

"Not to add any pressure, but it would give you the opportunity you've always wanted to start a homework club."

The idea had formed after the library started a mentoring program for the local high school students. She thought it would help build the foundation for success if they engaged the children when they were younger.

Clara slipped a paper between the pages of Julian Mayfield's *The Hit*, which Bailey had checked out, and pushed it across the desk. Bailey rolled her eyes when she recognized the job application.

"I'd hate to see what you consider pressure," she said snatching up the book. She stepped back and collided with Matteo, having forgotten he was standing behind her.

"What are you considering, Shorty?" he asked.

"Nothing." A job at the library was tempting, but it seemed foolish to consider after four years of studying to be an accountant. "What are you doing here?" she asked as they strolled out of the building. "And what did you say to Janet?"

Matteo's brow furrowed.

"The short librarian who doesn't look old enough to be in high school much less hold a job?"

His smirk returned, and Bailey suspected she would be apologizing to the woman next week.

"I told her I was going back to school and I needed a tutor."

Bailey pssted. The man had earned a bachelor's degree in mathematics by the time he was twenty and could calculate a column of numbers in his mind before she finished typing the first figure into a calculator. "And what do you expect to be tutored in? Sewing?" She flicked the loose button on his shirt.

"It's a useful skill."

"So is giving someone a straight answer. What are you doing here?"

"Thought I'd join you for story time. It *is* a public library."

"Matteo—"

"Okay." He chuckled. "I wanted to see how Norma was feeling."

Bailey pointed to the girl, who was walking ahead of them. A small audience tagged behind Norma, listening to her summarize *Alice's Adventures in Wonderland*, which she read after she finished *The Borrowers*.

"She was in bed until it was time to leave. Another good night's sleep and she'll be racing the boys down the street again."

"You think she'll be up to Coney Island this weekend?"

Bailey shook her head. "I don't want her excited."

"Then how about a picnic? We'll eat, relax, and get back early."

The correct answer would have been "No." As long as his family refused to acknowledge his existence, he was off limits. Yet, despite the reasons she could not go, Bailey nodded.

His wide grin told her he'd been certain her answer would be what he wanted.

"You're so sure of yourself," she mumbled.

"It's called confidence," he replied.

"I prefer 'cocky.' "

He shrugged his shoulders.

Bailey hastened her step to catch up with Norma, ignoring the chuckle behind her.

****

Her mood changed in a heartbeat. Their playful banter switched to seething rage and the stove was forced to suffer the consequences of his question when she slammed the frying pan onto the burner.

Matteo had not really wanted to know how Kyle was doing. Yet he figured, as a friend, he should inquire about her relationships and then feign happiness for her. But her reaction piqued his interest.

Bailey marched to the refrigerator and retrieved a package of meat. She shoved the door with enough force it bounced back open.

Matteo pushed away from the wall and closed the door, then followed her and placed a hand on her shoulder. He noticed the chain the other man had given her was no longer around her neck.

"What happened?" he asked.

Bailey dropped the food onto the counter and shook her head. Her ragged sigh and the silence that followed made him certain he would have to seek out the other man and get justice for her.

As Matteo was preparing to ask for Kyle's address, she sighed again. "He wanted me to choose between spending the night with him and taking care of my baby."

What the hell had the man been thinking? They had been together for two years. He should have known what her answer would be.

"What did he do?" Matteo asked.

She glanced back at the bedroom. Two feet peeped from underneath the bed, where Norma searched for clues in her quest to be a detective. Considering Bailey's penchant for cleaning, Matteo suspected the girl would not find as much as a speck of dust.

Thanks to his daughter, he was familiar with children's ability to absorb information, even when their attention seemed to be occupied by something else. He took Bailey's hand and led her to the back yard and closed the door.

"What did he do?" Matteo repeated.

"He found company elsewhere." She took a ragged breath and jerked her head towards the front of the house. "I caught him walking out of her building yesterday morning."

Matteo did not need her to elaborate on whose house the man exited. Bailey's blonde-haired neighbor had never been shy in expressing her interest in the opposite sex. And the woman did not discriminate. She flirted with him as much as she did with her tanner neighbors.

Matteo's fists itched to beat sense into the other man. How could someone throw away a chance to be with a good woman and a sweet child for a piece of ass half the neighborhood had sampled?

"What is wrong with me?" Bailey muttered.

He unclenched his fists as his frustration at the other man gave way to sympathy for her. "Nothing's wrong with you." He tugged on her arm until she stepped close enough for him to wrap himself around her.

"I have the worst taste in men." He strained to hear the words muffled by his chest. "There was Jose, who assumed, 'cause I had a child, I'd sleep with him on the first date. Then there was Ted, who wanted me to drop out of school and be a proper housewife." She sucked her teeth. "And I can't forget Norma's father. I told him I was pregnant, and he took off so fast he probably hit Florida before I made it back to my parents' farm from his."

Yes, her track record was not exactly stellar. She tended to attract losers who were not worth the efforts she put into building relationships with them.

Matteo kissed her forehead to offer comfort and relay his sympathy. The energy between them suddenly shifted. There was a pull that, no matter how hard he tried, he could not fight…not that he wanted to.

They were repeating the scenario they had visited three years earlier when his wife left his bags, along with divorce papers, outside his house. Too dazed to figure out which direction to turn, Matteo had showed up on Bailey's doorstep. As a friend, she welcomed him inside—and offered him a shoulder to lean on. But when she kissed his temple, she awakened a desire for her.

Matteo hooked a finger under Bailey's chin and tilted her head back. In the second before he lowered his head, he saw the desire in her eyes.

Their lips crushed against each other, and the jolt to his system said the memory he had been carrying from their last kiss had not been an illusion. His heart raced and he became aware of every nerve.

Hers was a kiss that made him want more. But what he craved and what he could get were two different things.

Being with her would not be a reality. Not only was he off-limits to her, but she also had just gotten out of a relationship. She was hurting, and he was taking advantage of that pain.

Matteo forced himself to break the kiss and step back from her. He stared at her slightly parted lips and shook his head.

"You're right. You have the worst taste in men…present company included."

Chapter Ten

The bell chimed and Bailey's head snapped up. Her spirits sank as a pair of teenagers strolled hand in hand into the diner, reminding her of a couple in the midst of their first love.

"Is something wrong?" Anita asked.

Belatedly, Bailey realized she'd emitted the mournful sigh of one pining away for a lover. She mentally slapped herself. Where was her self-respect? She had no business longing for a man who had pushed her away…not once, but twice.

"Having trouble breaking in these shoes." She sighed a second time hoping her boss couldn't tell the difference between a mournful sigh and one released out of frustration.

The knuckles perched on Anita's hip, her pursed lips, and her raised eyebrow said she would sooner believe the occurrences in "Hey, Diddle-Diddle" had actually happened than her employee's lie. Bailey, however, was not inclined to change her reply.

She placed two singles in the register and fished three quarters from the tray. She closed the drawer and held the change out to the gentleman seated at the counter.

He waved the money away as he slipped off the stool. Bailey dropped the coins into the front pocket of her apron.

The man's exit left only the couple, who were being waited on by her colleague. "If you don't need me for anything else, I have to go."

Anita's forehead furrowed. She glanced at the clock mounted on the far wall over the jukebox that was playing "There Goes My Baby." The wrinkles smoothed as the realization of what day it was flickered in her eyes. "Ah, yes, Norma's play." She pointed to the bouquet of roses under the counter. "Don't forget to take those for the star."

Bailey grabbed the flowers and slipped into the back room. She changed into a cream dress and matching shoes, smoothed her hair, and applied lipstick. After a quick check in the mirror, she rushed out to catch the bus.

She could not be late to the performance—not after missing the Christmas show to take her Advanced Accounting final. Norma had said she understood, and Nicholas and Georgia had attended the production, yet Bailey still carried the guilt for missing the event.

Her anxiety would not allow her to relax until she passed through the green-painted metal door into the auditorium brimming with bodies. There were only twenty-five children in Norma's class, yet it looked like every immediate, distant, and long-lost relative came out for the show.

Bailey stood in the back, scanning the crowd for an empty seat. During her second pass, she spied an empty seat halfway down on the left side of the room. She took two steps, then froze when she recognized red hair on the occupant next to the chair.

Eleanor Santiano. Matteo's ex-wife.

Though the women had attended many Santiano gatherings since 1951, they had not spoken more than five words to each other. Bailey realized she was partially to blame for the estrangement.

Not long after she would arrive at an event, Matteo would be by her side. They would spend hours talking about anything and everything, only stopping when a toast would be made or one of them was preparing to leave for the night. She should not have encouraged him. After a quick exchange of pleasantries, she should have sent him back to his wife's side. But it felt good to have someone pay attention to her.

Bailey shifted her search for a seat to the opposite end of the room. She located a chair with a sweater tossed over the back. Taking a chance, she made her way down the aisle while praying no one reached it before her.

She stopped at the end of the row, grasped the back of the seat, and cleared her throat to attract the attention of the slim blonde who was gossiping with a brunette. "Excuse me, is this seat taken?"

"No, it's free," the blonde said. "You can take—" The woman's upper lip curled back in contempt when she peered over her shoulder. "I was mistaken. This seat is taken. You might find something in the back of the room."

Bailey bristled at the woman's suggestion, yet bit back the retort on the tip of her tongue. As tempting as it was to give the woman a piece of her mind, she had to consider potential fallout. At best, the administrators would escort Bailey from the school, and she would miss the performance. At worst, the teachers could retaliate against Norma and refuse to let her participate in future events.

Without a word, Bailey headed back up the aisle and

sat in an available seat in the last row. No sooner had she settled in than the fairer couple next to her moved over, leaving an empty seat between them. On the opposite end of the auditorium, the families of the two other colored children sat in the second to last row.

Bailey was preparing to face forward when Matteo slipped through the door. The lights dimmed before she could raise a hand and wave him over.

Despite the fifteen yards separating them, she saw the tear that ran down his cheek when a girl with auburn curls walked on stage next to Norma. A lot could be said about the man, but one thing no one could deny was his love for his child.

As much as she wanted to comfort him, Bailey knew her words would not be an adequate substitute for his daughter's hug or whispered, "I love you, Daddy." She therefore returned her focus to the children as they marched onto the stage for the opening number.

Norma, one of only three colored children in the class of twenty-five, was seated so far off to the side of the stage she was practically hidden behind the curtain. Yet when she spoke, every syllable could be heard clearly. Yes, they may have placed her in the shadows, but they could not silence her.

When the performance was over, the parents gave the children a standing ovation. Beaming with pride, the little ladies curtsied, and the young gentlemen bowed before they proceeded backstage.

Bailey picked up Norma's roses and headed to the corridor where the parents had been instructed to wait for the children. Though he had been standing in the rear of the auditorium, Matteo got caught in the crowd and was unable to make it to the door before a girl surrounded by a pink cloud from her waist to her calves barreled down the hall. Her high-pitched squeal captured the attention of every parent, including the woman Matteo would have done better avoiding.

****

Tears rushed to Matteo's eyes as his daughter clung to his waist. There were a lot of things he regretted in his past, but making this girl would never be one of them.

He peered into the auditorium at his ex. The crowd had slowed her approach up the aisle. He had a minute—maybe two—before she reached him and dragged their daughter away, and he intended to take advantage of every second.

"Did you see the performance, Daddy?" Julia asked.

"Every moment."

Her broad smile revealed two missing top teeth.

"When did you lose your teeth?"

His daughter pointed to the space on the right. "I lost this one last week." She moved her finger to the left. "And I lost this one the week before."

"Did the tooth fairy leave you anything?"

"She left me five cents each time."

Considering how much the tooth fairy walked away with in the divorce, she could have left a dime for each tooth.

Matteo pulled out his wallet and passed her two dollars. "Here's a little extra something."

"Thank you, Daddy."

As he shoved the wallet into his back pocket, he remembered another gift he had for her. While he had not expected to speak to her, he had grabbed it off his dresser, just in case. He crouched in front of her and pulled a gold heart pendant and chain out of the front pocket of his shirt.

"I'm sorry I missed your birthday."

Julia cupped the pendant in her hand. "This matches the bracelet Uncle Louie gave me."

Considering her mother had no siblings and none of Matteo's three brothers were named Louie, he wondered who the girl was referring to. Before he could question her, Julia was yanked back.

"What the hell are you doing here?" Eleanor demanded.

Matteo's gaze moved up a shapely calf to a narrow waist, and then a pair of full breasts that would make a man initially overlook a personality flaw.

With a sigh, he stood up and glowered at the woman, whose red dress accentuated all her curves and had men stopping and staring despite the presence of their wives. Had he not been thinking with his dick instead of his brain years earlier, he would not have missed the downward turn of her lips, the wrinkled nose, or the cold blue eyes that disapprovingly bore into him whenever he was in her presence.

"I came to see my daughter perform," he replied.

"You lost all rights to call her that when you chose that junk over us."

Whoever said "words could never hurt" had never been told he did not have the right to claim his child. Ripping open his chest and tearing out his heart would have inflicted less pain than he felt at that moment.

Matteo would not argue that he'd messed up…from lying with Eleanor without a glove to thinking marriage would solve everything and then turning to drugs when it did not. However, through it all, he always loved his daughter.

He swallowed the lump in the back of his throat and glared through his unshed tears. "Just let me give Julia this, and I'll leave you alone." He held up the locket.

"She doesn't need anything from you."

Matteo grabbed her arm as she took a step to go around him. "Eleanor—"

"You've always been hardheaded."

His focus shifted past his ex-wife to the man who earned the distinction of becoming an ex-friend when he learned the man had been screwing one of his girlfriends in high school.

Louie Batanno had always coveted what Matteo had, from the lunchbox he carried in second grade to the shoes he wore in the seventh grade. But what the other man wanted most was a place in the Santiano family, along with the power and prestige that came with being associated them. He later learned his goal would never be achieved as, no matter how small, a betrayal was never rewarded.

If it had been only her, Matteo would not care who his ex-wife bedded. But he did not want his daughter calling that other man "Father," "Uncle," or any other term of endearment that did not include the words "jackass," "bastard," or "son-of-a-bitch."

"I don't want him around Julia," Matteo stated.

"You have no say in regard to who she's around," Eleanor replied.

"I'm her father."

His nemesis snorted. "With a father like you, she'd be better off a bastard."

A roar unlike any Matteo had ever heard from an animal or human screamed in his head. His hand ached from the tight ball of his fist.

"Matteo, no!"

The stern command and the hands on his chest broke his trance. His vision cleared and he stared at Bailey, who stood unflinching between him and the man he wanted to send to hell.

It had been dangerous for her to step between two men ready to rip into each other. Yet she showed no concern either man would insist on settling their disagreement with her standing there.

Bailey shoved a bag into one of his hands and a bouquet of roses into the other. "Take these and wait outside for me." She issued the command as if she had no doubt he would obey her.

Matteo wanted to drop the bag and flowers, pick Bailey up and set her to the side, and then face off against the other man. The disappointment in her eyes convinced him to back down for the first time in his life.

"Don't take too long," he said, stepping back.

Bailey dropped her hands from his chest and hurried down the hall. He watched until she disappeared around a corner before he glanced at Julia, who peeped from behind her mother's skirt.

"Remember, I love you, Sugarplum," he said softly. Not expecting the girl to reply, he turned towards the front door. Parents stepped to the side, making a path to the exit. A few men appeared disappointed they were not going to witness a fight. One muttered, "Punk," under his breath. Matteo, however, decided Bailey's opinion mattered more than that of those who saw him as less than a man for not only backing down to a woman, but a colored woman at that.

After everyone else had written him off, she offered him a second chance and hope his family would one day welcome him back. He would not ignore her wishes to satisfy the bloodthirst of those who would not give a damn about him once the show was over.

Matteo stopped at the corner. Seconds later, Louie emerged from the building with an arm around Eleanor's shoulders. Julia walked behind the couple and climbed into the back seat of the black Cadillac convertible. The girl's eyes locked on his. She mouthed, "I love you, too," behind her mother's back. She raised her hand an inch off her lap and waved to him as the car drove past him.

He waited until the vehicle was in the next block before he acknowledged the woman who had laid a hand on his arm to alert him to her presence.

"What were you thinking?" Bailey asked.

The right answer was that he hadn't been thinking at all, or at least not realistically. In his fantasy, Julia would run to him and, after seeing how much his daughter meant to him, Eleanor would concede and allow him back in Julia's life. But just like elephants did not forget, neither did bitter ex-wives who were determined not to forgive.

Matteo passed the bouquet to Norma. "Here, these are from…" he paused, unwilling to take credit for someone else's gift.

"Anita," Bailey added.

"I'm sorry for ruining your evening."

Norma took the flowers. "I forgive you." The girl uttered the words he hoped to hear one day from his daughter.

"Lately, there's a lot you should be sorry for," Bailey said.

He knew she was referring to the kiss. Yes, he was sorry—not about the kiss but about walking out on her.

It was not a topic he was willing to discuss in front of an audience, particularly one with big ears and an impressionable mind.

She grasped the bag hanging from his arm. The streetlight illuminated the emerald and diamonds in the ring decorating the third finger of Bailey's right hand. His grandmother had promised he could have the jewelry for his bride. Yet when he was ready to give it to Eleanor, he remembered, Nonna had refused to hand it over.

Matteo always assumed his grandmother disapproved of Eleanor because she had gotten pregnant out of wedlock. However, not only had Bailey gotten pregnant before she recited vows, but she also had never changed her marital status.

There was a good explanation as to how Bailey came into possession of the jewelry. And while Matteo could not come up with one, he was certain she had not stolen it.

Deciding it was neither the time nor the place to broach the subject, Matteo said, "I'll carry this for you."

"Come on then." She reached back for Norma.

The girl grasped her mother's hand and they headed in the direction of her apartment.

"You were good," he told Norma. "I'm sorry I didn't think to bring you flowers. How 'bout I make it up to you when we go out Sunday?"

"Where are we going?"

"A picnic. How does that sound?"

The girl's face brightened. "I bet I could find more clues."

Matteo recalled the girl's interest in Nancy Drew and his childhood desire to become a sleuth and experience adventures once he read the Hardy Boys.

Hoping the girl could enjoy playing pretend for as long as possible, he questioned her about the clues she had already discovered. Their play ended abruptly when they entered her apartment, and a harsh reality greeted them.

"Where were you?" Lincoln demanded from the sofa he was sprawled across, sans pants.

"I should be asking you that." Bailey blocked Norma from cutting through the living room and pointed towards the kitchen. "And what did I tell you 'bout paradin' your business around here."

Matteo stepped into the living room and closed the door that divided the space from the bedroom.

Lincoln glanced at his crotch. "Ain't nothin' showin'."

"I don't care." She picked up a pair of pants and held them out to him. "Put those on...*now*."

Her brother sucked his teeth and huffed as he snatched the pants from her and shoved a foot into a leg.

"So, where were you?" Lincoln asked.

"Tonight was your niece's school play," Bailey replied.

Lincoln pulled the pants over the other foot. "Dammit, I forgot." He stood up and tucked his shirt in at the waist. "Hey, Busy Bee, I'm sorry I missed your recital."

"That's okay, Uncle Lincoln."

From Matteo's perspective, it was not okay. For the second time that night, the girl had to accept an apology. She could not grow up believing it was okay for the men in her life to mess up and an apology would make things right.

"I left you some Chinese food on the stove." Lincoln

sniffed and wiped his nose with the back of his hand.

"At least you did something around here." She pointed to the blankets tossed on the sofa.

"A *thank you* would be nice. I didn't have to buy you anythin'."

"Thank you, but I'd also appreciate it if you'd pick up after yourself."

"Okay, fine." Lincoln yanked up the zipper on the front of his pants and snatched his jacket off the chair. "I'll do it later. I gotta go. I'll see you later, Busy Bee. I'm proud of you." Without acknowledging his sister, Lincoln walked out.

Shaking her head, Bailey dropped her purse on the paper-covered coffee table. "Are you staying for dinner?"

Matteo wanted to take Bailey up on her offer. There was so much they needed to discuss—from the kiss to his suspicions about her brother's drug use. But he also needed time to consider the best way to broach the topics. A half-assed explanation could end all future invitations.

"A raincheck?" He moved to her side, grasped her shoulders and leaned in.

The memory of his last time at the house flashed in his mind. If he followed through with the peck to her forehead there was no doubt it would lead to more...a more intense kiss, more cravings and more regrets.

Matteo dropped his hands to his side and stepped around Bailey. Breaking their last kiss was hard, but walking out of the apartment now was arduous. He would have to figure out a way to be around her and control himself, as he refused to entertain the option of leaving her alone.

He stopped at the gate and gawked in disbelief as Lincoln exchanged a clear bag of what appeared to be oregano—though Matteo knew better—for a wad of cash with his blonde neighbor. Even without considering the transaction, the man should have been ashamed of himself for fraternizing with the woman who slept with his sister's man.

Matteo glowered at the couple until the woman jerked her head in his direction. Lincoln peered over his shoulder. He muttered something that did not travel back to Matteo's ears before walking off.

"Wait up." Matteo's command was in vain. By the time a car passed, allowing him to jog across the street, the man had disappeared around the corner.

Matteo raced after Bailey's brother, finally catching up to him at the subway station.

"What do you need?" Lincoln asked without slowing his steps when Matteo reached his side. "I've got things to do."

"How could you associate with that woman after what she did to your sister?" Matteo asked.

"Who I talk to is my business."

"She slept with your sister's man."

"How's that concern me?"

"Family comes first."

"You're a fine one to talk." Lincoln sniffed, then rubbed his thumb across his nose. "Your family won't have anythin' to do with you."

It was for that reason Matteo needed to get the other man to understand there were few things that hurt more than being on the outs with one's family.

"So, whacha on?" Matteo asked.

Lincoln shoved his hands in his pants pockets.

"Don't know what you're talking 'bout."

"You're using. You've got all the signs."

"Just 'cause you're a junkie doesn't mean everyone else is usin'." With a snort, Lincoln stopped under a streetlight and glared back with bloodshot eyes. "You worry about your shit and leave me the hell alone."

Lincoln marched away, signifying the conversation was over. He had gotten defensive but never denied he was using. In Matteo's experience, that was an admission of guilt.

The man's reaction had not been much different from Matteo's when his father confronted him. Though he was using more and more junk every day and it had affected his family and was close to ruining his friendship with Bailey, he'd refused to admit he had a problem. It was only after he had the snot kicked out of him and was left bleeding on the side of the road outside the city that he realized how far he had fallen.

If history was about to repeat itself, but with a new set of players, Bailey needed to be warned. He was not sure how to break the news to her or whether she would believe him. He only knew she had to be told as soon as possible.

By the time he stepped off his bus, Matteo had not gotten any closer on deciding how to approach Bailey. He just knew help would be needed in the event there was trouble.

The neighborhood had started to settle down for the evening. The businesses had closed for the evening. Fathers had returned home from work. Children had gone inside to prepare for bed.

In the building next to his, a mother fussed at her children, who had yet to complete their homework.

Lawrence Welk blasted from Mrs. Murphy's apartment.

Having taken care of all his chores before he left for the school, Matteo headed straight for his apartment. The air downstairs was thick with cigarette smoke. It was not until he pushed open his door that he realized the stench was too fresh; he had not smoked a cigarette in the apartment since lunch.

Matteo noted the shadow next to the door and swung. A nose shifted under his fist. A man yowled. And a body slammed back against the wall.

It was the only blow he had the pleasure of landing.

Hands grabbed him from behind. The light from the hall cast a yellow glow over Louie's distorted features. He did not utter a word, not that he needed to. The fist he rammed into Matteo's gut relayed the man's disgust at having bumped into his enemy earlier. And the blow to his left eye was a warning as to what else Matteo could expect if he tried to contact his ex-wife or daughter again.

His nemesis failed to realize, though, that Matteo was too hardheaded to heed the lesson. He would never stop trying to make sure Julia understood how much he cared for her.

Chapter Eleven

"I need your help," Matteo announced when the front door to his uncle's brownstone opened.

Growing up, he'd thought asking for help was a sign of weakness. A real man handled his problems and didn't need to turn to anyone else. But concern for Bailey and Norma now pushed aside his pride. If he wanted to protect them, he couldn't do it on his own.

Thankfully, the woman who answered the door showed no scorn for his statement or disgust at his presence. Instead, Nonna opened her arms and welcomed him into a familial embrace.

As a child, Matteo would sit on his grandmother's lap and inhale the five-and-dime lilac scent she favored over the more expensive perfumes her sons gave her over the years. When he became too old for such babyish behavior, he would give her a two-second hug and a quick peck on the cheek before running off to join his cousin in whatever mischief they could find. But, after being denied the opportunity to simply wave to the woman from across the street, he was not in a hurry to pull away from her.

"*Piccolo*, I've missed you," Nonna said, referring to him by the nickname she had not used since he started school.

"I've missed you too, Nonna," he confessed.

The embrace lasted longer than a heartbeat, but he

felt the void when she pulled back. He would never take another hug for granted.

"Are you through using that junk?"

"Yes, ma'am." His ears burned with the shame of having this conversation with her.

"That's good." She pinched his face in her hand and examined his black eye. "I take it Eleanor wasn't happy to see you."

"You know about last night?"

"She called, accusing Bailey of stealing my ring."

Though he hadn't figured out how she got the ring, he refused to believe Bailey would take it. "Nonna, she would never—"

"I know she didn't, 'cause I gave her the ring. Eleanor pitched a fit when I told her. Said the ring rightfully belonged to her. I reminded her it belonged to the person I chose to give it to."

"Why wouldn't you give it to me when I married her?"

"'Cause I never liked her." His grandmother stepped to the side and waved him into the house.

Matteo closed the door and followed her into the kitchen, lit only by the sunlight streaming through the open window next to the stove. She spent a lot of her time in this room, preparing meals, and always had something to offer guests whenever someone stopped by.

Nonna pointed to the chair pushed under the table set for two. When he was growing up, she had the ability to know, with one look, what mischief her grandchildren had gotten into. Despite her 'gift,' she was not psychic. He could therefore surmise she had made lunch for someone other than him.

Before Matteo could protest, his grandmother's eyes narrowed, silently warning him it would be in his best interest not to argue with her. Not wanting to risk displeasing her so soon after being welcomed, he pulled out the chair and sat.

"I promised to give you the ring when you found the right woman—and Eleanor wasn't her," Nonna said. "That girl spent years chasing the men in this family, trying to get her hooks into someone. It didn't matter who, as long as he made her a Santiano. You just happened to be the one she caught."

More like he had been the only one stupid enough to take her for a ride without a glove. It wasn't like he hadn't known what a condom was or how to use it. His father had expounded the importance of keeping himself covered until he was ready to get married.

"Why did you give the ring to Bailey?" he asked.

"'Cause she's the right woman."

"But how—"

She winked at him. "You told me."

Matteo wondered if his grandmother was losing it. He had never discussed his feelings for Bailey with anyone.

"Your demeanor always changed whenever she entered the room. You were more relaxed and more attentive to her."

It was easy to relax around someone who wasn't demanding or complaining about every little thing. Unlike Eleanor, Bailey took an interest in him, not what he could provide.

Still, he could not do anything about it. He was an outcast and, to be with him, Bailey would have to go against her family.

It was the same estrangement that also limited the protection Matteo was able to give Bailey. Most of his connections were loyal to the Santiano family. They would not help him while he was disowned. However, if the same poison that had controlled him had the potential of harming someone in the family, his cousin would do what was necessary to protect them.

"I need to speak to Nick," Matteo said.

"Nicky would sooner stand by and watch someone cut your heart out than help you," Celeste said.

Startled by the unexpected declaration, Matteo shifted in his seat to face his cousin, who stood in the doorway with her arms crossed over her chest and her cold, hard glare boring into him.

The youngest grandchild and only granddaughter of Buddy and Sophie Santiano, Celeste was considered the princess of the family. It had been the responsibility of all the cousins to protect her. Yet Matteo had been too busy destroying his life to live up to his responsibility.

Yes, there were several others, including Celeste's own brother, who had failed to recognize the demon her husband had been. However, Matteo still wondered whether the results would have been different if he had been clean and able to focus on someone other than himself.

"What have you done now?" Celeste's emotionless voice chilled him.

"It's not for me." Not ready to put all Bailey's business out there, he only added, "It's for a friend."

"Is she in danger?" his grandmother asked.

"I'm not sure." Despite the tantrums he'd witnessed, there was no guarantee Lincoln would lash out at Bailey.

"You must've thought it was important, to come

here. I'll let Nick know you're looking for him."

"He can reach me at—"

"I'm sure he already knows how to find you."

Matteo nodded. It was his cousin's ability to keep track of his enemies that made speaking to him essential.

His grandmother placed two plates of chicken and pasta on the table. "Sit, *Bambina*. Eat."

"I'm not hungry," Celeste said.

"I didn't ask."

Celeste dropped her arms to her side, dragged her feet across the black-and-white linoleum, and dropped into the chair opposite Matteo. Yes, her appearance and disposition had gone through a drastic change, but no, she had not lost her respect for her elders.

Matteo shuddered at the teeth-clenching squeal of Celeste's fork against her plate. She kept her head bowed as she dug into the food she had not wanted to eat.

When all the lies, thefts, and drugs came to light, Nicholas had been charged with doling out the punishment that reminded Matteo of the consequences of screwing over the family. Yet the physical pain from his punishment paled in comparison to the pain of his family disowning him.

The doorbell rang and Celeste dropped her fork. Nonna pushed the younger woman back into the chair as she passed by the table. Matteo received a pat on his back before she left the cousins alone.

"Why did you do it?" The voice that asked the question was so soft it was nearly drowned out by the murmurs from the floor over them.

Matteo watched his cousin, whose gaze returned to her plate. He realized she was not only trying to learn what possessed him to turn to drugs but get answers about her husband's demons.

He could not answer for the other man, as every user had a different reason for turning to drugs. All he could do was speak about his experience. "I wanted to forget."

Celeste raised her head. "Forget what? Your vows? Your responsibilities?"

"Yes." Matteo knew the answer would not redeem him in her eyes, yet she deserved the truth. "Living with Eleanor was like serving a life sentence, and I needed something to help me get through the day."

"An unhappy marriage is supposed to excuse everything?"

"No, it's not. I'm also not looking for sympathy, 'cause I knew it was wrong before I snorted my first line."

"Why'd you come back?"

Matteo had been left battered and high on the side of the road with instructions not to return. But he could not bring himself to stay away from his daughter.

"While I never loved her mother, Julia's my heart. I want to be close to her."

"After everything you did, you expect things to go back to the way they were?"

Matteo shook his head. He knew he could not show up and expect Eleanor to let him be a part of Julia's life. He needed to earn her trust, and it would take time.

****

The man stood out like a dog in a roomful of cats. No matter how hard he tried to appear nonchalant, leaning against the 1956 green sedan, with his fair complexion and tailored suit, he was unable to blend in with the environment.

Bailey's heart skipped a beat when she spotted him

outside her building. Her instincts screamed nothing good was going to come from a confrontation with him. She wanted to avoid him, but she knew he would not be put off. He would continue to return until he spoke with her.

"Good evening, Mr. Petersen," she called out when she was three yards from the principal of Norma's school.

The man looked up from the folder he was skimming through. His furrowed brow and clenched jaw further hinted at news she'd rather not hear.

Bailey's gaze shifted to Norma, who stood on the first step leading to the upper apartment. The girl's eyes were wide with worry and confusion.

"Miss Collins, I wish to speak to you about your daughter." His baritone voice carried down the block, piquing the curiosity of any neighbor interested in sticking a nose in her business.

Deciding she would rather have some control over what information the neighbors got, she waved towards the building.

"Please come inside."

The man pushed away from the car and followed her inside. Too late, she decided she preferred her neighbors to overhear the conversation than have the man judge her for the chaos her brother had left behind.

"We can talk in the kitchen."

He peered into the living room, where clothes were scattered across every piece of furniture, before following Bailey. Her ears burned with shame. She had continually reminded Lincoln the room he was crashing in was the first space everyone saw when they entered the apartment and the state of it went a long way in the opinions people formed of them.

She stepped into the kitchen and prayed the floor would open and swallow her when the ripe garbage assaulted her senses. The man's wrinkled nose conveyed his opinion about her housekeeping skills.

Believing no excuse would change his mind, Bailey waved at a chair.

Mr. Petersen was still lowering himself to the chair when he announced, "Mrs. Santiano stopped by to inform me that the address we have on file for your daughter is incorrect. In fact, neither you nor Norma have every lived there."

The pit crashed in Bailey's stomach. Since the day Matteo suggested she use his address so Norma could attend the same school as Julia, she'd lived in fear of someone discovering the truth.

"Do you deny the allegations?" Mr. Petersen asked.

Doing so would be fruitless. His presence in her kitchen confirmed part of what Eleanor had said was true. All he needed to do was ask her neighbors when she'd moved in or inquire if anyone in Eleanor's neighborhood knew her to confirm the other charge.

"No, I don't. But I can explain—"

"Miss Collins, there are over one million students in the New York City Public Schools. To keep order, the system is divided into districts, which are further divided into zones. We cannot have people placing their children into whatever zone they choose."

"I know, but—"

"Then you can understand why, effective immediately, your daughter has been expelled."

The pit jumped in her stomach, upsetting the food that should have settled there hours earlier. Bailey had known sneaking Norma into the school was wrong, but she wanted her daughter to get a good education.

Despite the assurances by the city that all the children received equal opportunities, she had seen the battered, outdated textbooks used by the students who attended the schools in colored neighborhoods. And based on the homework assignments she had seen some of the children working on at the library, she knew the colored schools were behind the others.

"The children only have a couple more weeks 'til summer vacation," Bailey said. "Couldn't she finish out the year with her class and then enroll in her zone school next year?"

"I've taken the liberty of dropping off her records at her new school." Mr. Petersen continued as if she had not asked the question. "The principal was not in, so I'm not sure how he will feel about your daughter starting this late in the school year." He removed a paper from his folder and pushed it across the table. "This is their address."

"Could she finish off the week and say goodbye to her friends?" They only had one more day.

He pushed up from the table. "Miss Collins, I hope things work out for you," he said. "I'll see myself out."

Bailey watched his retreating back and silently willed him to turn back and announce he'd changed his mind. Her plea turned to prayer when the man could no longer be seen. The prayer switched to bargaining with higher powers when the front door clicked closed. It all turned to despair when the roaring engine of his vehicle faded.

Just when she had thought Norma had the foundation she needed to move up in the world, another obstacle had been thrown in their way.

A movement pulled Bailey's attention from the paper she had unintentionally crumpled in her fist. She held a hand out to Norma, who cowered in the shadows outside the entrance.

"Come here, Busy Bee." Her tone soft, despite her urge to scream in frustration.

Norma dragged her feet until she stood in front her mother. Bailey pulled the girl onto her lap and held her tight, trying to draw strength from the child who had been an inspiration since she came into the world.

"Sometimes people fib to help others. Though their heart is in the right place, if the truth is discovered, they are still punished."

Norma tilted her head and raised an eyebrow like Bailey had done so many times. She should not have expected the girl to understand such a cryptic explanation for the visit. Just as she would expect the girl not to beat around the bush when confronted, she needed to confess her sins without hesitation.

Bailey took a deep breath, then forced herself to lead by example.

"I used Julia's address so you could go to the same school as her." Yes, Matteo had made the suggestion, but she had ultimately agreed to go along with the scheme. Therefore, she would not shift the blame. "Your principal found out and he is sending you to another school."

"But I don't want to go to another school," Norma said.

"I know, Busy Bee, but we don't have a choice."

"Please, Mommy?" The dam opened and a flood of tears spilled from the girl's eyes. "I promise I'll behave.

I won't race the boys when the teachers aren't looking. Or yell out the answers without raising my hand."

"Sweetie, you didn't do anything wrong." Bailey hugged the girl. She should have known she would not get away with conning the system.

"Tomorrow we were gonna have a spelling bee, and next week we were going to the park."

"I'm sure they'll do that at your new school."

"I don't want to do it with them. I want to do it with my class."

Norma buried her head in her mother's shoulder. Her sobs broke Bailey's heart.

Bailey had wanted the best for her daughter. But, thanks to her scheming, she'd ended up breaking the child's heart.

She rocked Norma until the tears stopped flowing. Afterwards, she made dinner, which, in hindsight, was a waste of time. Norma picked at the food on her plate for twenty minutes before complaining of a stomachache. Having lost her own appetite, Bailey didn't blame the child for not wanting to eat and excused her from the table.

In the need for an outlet for her anger and disappointment over the situation, Bailey washed the dishes and scrubbed the kitchen floor. Yet, aside from making the linoleum shine, the chore did nothing for her. It neither solved her problem nor did it make her feel better.

With a sigh, she grabbed the garbage bag and started towards the front door. She glanced at her disheveled living room and was tempted to shove the clothes into the bag, as the owner could not care too much for his belongings if he simply left them strewn over the room.

Bailey shook her head. Money was too hard to come by for her to throw away good clothes.

She deposited the garbage in the first of two metal trash cans sitting in the corner of the front yard. When she stepped back into the house, she could no longer ignore the mess in her front room.

She snatched the two shirts she had ironed for Lincoln on Monday off the chair. He had begged her to help him out when she was pressing Norma's dresses, claiming he needed to look sharp. But her work had been for naught if he was not going to hang up his clothes to keep the wrinkles from settling back in.

With the shirts draped over her arm, she continued to move around the room, adding a pair of pants and three ties to the pile.

She reached the sofa and shook her head at the bedsheet balled in the corner. Growing up, her brothers never made a bed, as the chore fell on Bailey, who had to complete the task before she left for school each morning. Yet she would have thought Lincoln, after ten years in the Army, would have not only picked up the skill but maintained the habit after he was discharged.

Uncertain as to the last time he'd washed the sheet, she decided to toss it in the laundry basket and replace it with a fresh one.

Bailey grabbed the bedsheet and tucked it under her arm. As she reached for a blue throw pillow Georgia had made from two washcloths, a glint of black caught her attention. She dropped the pillow back onto the floor where her brother had kicked it and pulled the gun from between the sofa cushions.

Her heart chilled.

How could her brother be so irresponsible as to

leave the weapon lying around where her daughter could find it? She shuddered as she imagined the consequences that could have occurred if Norma had come across the weapon and her curiosity had gotten the best of her.

"What are you doing with my shit?"

Bailey jumped at her brother's question. Lincoln stood in the threshold of the room, His nostrils flared, his hands balled in fists, and his chest rose and fell in a barely controlled rage.

Her own anger grew. He had some nerve, getting upset at her when he was the one who had put her daughter in jeopardy. Plus, she would never have found the gun if he had cleaned up behind himself.

"I'm cleaning my living room," she replied. "I don't need anyone walking in here, judging me 'cause of your sh—" She barely caught the curse before it spilled from her lips. She took a deep breath and quickly counted back from ten to one to get control of her tongue. Norma had already been through enough that evening. She did not need to hear her mother cursing like a sailor.

Once she believed she could continue without the profanity, she asked, "Why do you have a gun?"

"It's none of your damn business." Lincoln stepped up to her, grabbed the barrel, and snatched the weapon from her hand.

Their father had taught them how to properly handle guns before they turned ten and, she suspected, her brother had been given a refresher course when he was in the service. Therefore, his recklessness with the weapon made her even more determined that he would get rid of it.

"I want that out my apartment," Bailey said.

"I thought this was *our* apartment."

"You want something you can call your own, then get a place with *your* name on the lease. Until then, this is *my* apartment, and I don't want guns lying around where Norma can get to them."

"Fine, I'll get rid of it in the morning." He placed the weapon on the end table.

"No, you're gonna get rid of it now."

Lincoln scowled at her.

Determined, she faced him, unflinching, until he emitted a low growl and shoved the barrel of the gun into the waistband of his pants.

"Fine, I'll get rid of it." He marched out of the room, buttoning his jacket to conceal the weapon.

Bailey remained planted in her spot until the front door closed and the gate clanged shut. Assured he did not simply place the gun in the trash can but was abiding by her wishes, she tossed the bedsheet and clothes onto the chair. She yanked the cushions off the sofa and searched for any more surprises her brother had stashed in the furniture.

By the time she was finished, the living room looked worse than before she had decided to straighten up. To her relief, she had not uncovered anything else that could put her daughter in danger.

The clock in a corner of the room chimed nine times, reminding her she would need to get up early to take Norma to her new school and get her settled in. She quickly pushed the furniture back into place and gathered the clothes and linen she had previously picked up. As she was heading to the hall closet to hang up the shirts, there was a knock on the door.

Bailey peeped through the window and frowned at Matteo's bad timing.

151

"It's kind of late to be visiting," she said when she opened the door.

"I wanted to talk to you after Norma went to bed," Matteo said.

"Unfortunately, that's where I was heading."

"It's important."

"More important than Norma getting kicked out of school?"

Matteo flinched. "What happened?"

"Eleanor spoke to the principal and came clean about Norma's address."

"Damn, I'm sorry, Bailey." Matteo ran his hand through his hair. "Listen, I'll think of something."

She shook her head. Had he not insisted on trying to skirt the system, she would not be in the current situation. "It's not necessary."

"But—"

"No buts about it. I don't want your help."

She stepped back and slammed the door closed. She glanced at the clothes and linen in her arms. Tired of trying to fix the messes everyone else made, she tossed everything onto the floor and headed to the bedroom.

Chapter Twelve

"Why'd you do it?" Matteo asked when the mahogany door opened.

A smirk spread across Eleanor's face. He was flabbergasted. The woman was actually proud of getting Norma expelled.

"You took your anger out on a child simply because you didn't get a ring?"

Eleanor rolled her eyes. "This had nothing to do with that ring." She leaned against the doorjamb and examined the five perfectly manicured nails on her right hand. "Your grandmother can take it to hell with her for all I care."

Matteo stepped back from the woman to make certain he was out of arm's reach of her. Even when he was using he'd never laid a hand on her in anger. Yet her continued disrespect of his grandmother would have him adding another sin to his belt.

"Then why did you do it?" he asked. "What do you have against Norma?"

"I don't have anything against her." Eleanor lifted her head and hissed, "It's her mother I can't stand."

He tried to recall the few times Eleanor and Bailey had been in the same room together and what, if anything, the other woman could have done to antagonize his ex-wife. But try as he might, nothing came to mind. They barely exchanged pleasantries before Bailey joined his grandmother and mother in the kitchen. Meanwhile, Eleanor held court and gossiped with anyone willing to listen.

Matteo shook his head. "But why?"

"'Cause she had the one thing I always wanted," Eleanor replied.

The woman was making no sense. Compared to Eleanor, Bailey had nothing. In fact, most of her possessions were acquired after the more spoiled woman decided she no longer wanted them.

"You have money, a house, the latest fashion. What could she possible have that you don't?"

"You." Eleanor scrunched her face until it was distorted and grotesque.

"It's not like you ever wanted me." Matteo shook his head. "You only cared about my name."

"But I still tried to make you happy—at least in the beginning. When you came home from work, your favorite dinner was on the stove and the house was spotless. Hell, I tried to look good for you every evening."

Matteo wrinkled his forehead. He had to admit he never thought about the efforts she had put into the marriage. He simply thought the food was there because they had to eat, and he never noticed anything special in her appearance.

Eleanor snorted. "Did you really think after dealing with a colicky baby all day that I wanted to do my hair and put on makeup and dress up?" she asked as if she read his mind. "I did all that for you, and not once did you acknowledge my efforts." She threw her hands up in the air. "When *she* came along, it was like watching a lovestruck boy chasing after his first crush. We'd go to your uncle's place and you'd watch the door 'til she arrived. Then you'd run off and sit with her 'til it was time to leave. The only bright side was that you took Julia to play with her daughter and gave me the day off."

Matteo would admit his heart had never been in the marriage. He only stood before a preacher with her 'cause he thought that's what a man was supposed to do when he knocked up a woman. In hindsight, a real man wouldn't have banged someone he had no feelings for—or at least covered himself before doing the deed.

Still, there was no reason for Eleanor to be jealous of Bailey. "I never cheated on you with her."

"You never slept with her 'cause you had your other whores to scratch your itch." Eleanor hmphed. "No, *she* was the one who had your heart. You always turned to *her* when you had a problem or simply wanted to talk. I was left with a shell that barely grunted when I asked about his day."

Everything Eleanor said was the truth. He enjoyed the conversations he had with Bailey. They could spend the day talking and not run out of things to say.

Matteo glanced at the mother of his child. He had done a disservice not only to her but to Bailey, too. He had given his name to one, his heart to the other, and his body to a third.

The day he realized who owned his heart, he should have freed the woman he had been hitched to, forsaken the one he banged, and promised to love, honor and cherish the other.

"I'll admit I did you wrong and accept whatever punishment dealt to me in this life and the next. But our problems started before Bailey and Norma were in the picture. They are innocent and, from this moment on, off limits."

Matteo did not ask if she understood, nor did he

make a verbal promise of what would happen if she took her anger out on the wrong person again. Yet Eleanor straightened from her slouch and shifted from one foot to the other before she nodded her head, confirming she understood the consequences of messing with someone under the protection of the Santiano family.

****

Norma beamed at the five cents the customer had dropped into her palm after she handed him a menu. She had so many options as to what to do with her newly acquired wealth—she could either buy five pieces of gum or she could add it to the other tips she had earned throughout the day and go for a bigger purchase.

Bailey's spirits sank as she watched her daughter. She did not want the girl mesmerized by shiny coins that tempted the recipient with the little trinkets it could purchase. She wanted her daughter in school so she could one day earn much more for simply walking into an office.

The bell over the door chimed for what felt like the hundredth time that day. Reminding herself that Norma was too young to be the sole breadwinner in the family, Bailey grabbed a menu from under the counter. She glanced up to do the job she had been hired to perform, then froze when she saw Matteo.

He stood next to the door and frowned while watching Norma go to an empty table. She picked up a glass, pulled a rag from the apron tied around her waist, and wiped off the surface.

When Norma walked over to another table to collect a plate, he locked eyes with Bailey and held her gaze as if trying to gauge her reaction to his presence.

Bailey slapped a menu onto the counter and nodded

at the stool in front of her.

"Why didn't you enroll Norma in her zoned school this morning?" Matteo asked as he climbed onto the seat.

She crossed her arms over her chest and rolled her eyes.

"Okay, so you *did* take her to school. What happened?"

"The principal thought it would be best if I waited until the new school year to enroll her." She sucked her teeth. "Of course, he also hinted that with her missing close to three weeks of school, it may be in her best interest to repeat the second grade."

"Are you kidding me?"

Bailey pointed to her face. "Does this look like I'm kidding?"

"I'm sorry. This is all my fault." Matteo took her hand between both of his. "If I hadn't shown up at the school and argued with Louie, Eleanor wouldn't've ratted you out."

She shook her head. "It was only a matter of time before someone found out the truth about Norma's residence. I just need to get her into a school and then make sure she isn't left behind."

"You won't have anything to worry about. As smart as she is, Norma will have no problem proving she should be in the third grade."

"Now that she has dreams of going to college, I don't want anything holding her back."

"That, I can promise you, won't happen. She's like her mama...strong-willed and determined. Nothing's gonna stand in her way."

"Waitress." An older woman, sitting in the booth behind Matteo, held up an empty cup.

Bailey slipped her hand from Matteo's, grabbed the coffeepot, and approached the table. The diner, who was deep into a conversation with her companion, did not acknowledge her approach or express gratitude once the cup was filled.

"What do you plan to do with Norma during the day?" Matteo asked when she returned behind the counter.

"I haven't had a chance to think about it," Bailey replied as she set the pot down.

"If there's anything I can do—"

"I'll let you know," she insisted, knowing he would always be there for her.

Chapter Thirteen

The green-eyed monster was getting on Bailey's nerves.

No matter how hard she tried, jealousy gripped at her whenever she glanced across the room at Georgia, who sat surrounded by enough baby clothes to open a store. It was not so much the number of presents given to her by the expectant grandfathers, but the number of people who came out to celebrate the impending arrival of the newest addition to the household.

There had been no celebration for Bailey during her pregnancy. The first two months had been spent praying there was another explanation for the absence of her monthly visitor. When she could no longer avoid the truth, she had to deal with the vile names her parents hurled at her while they tossed her belongings out the door.

Though her uncle had taken her in, she'd had to find a job to support her and her baby while other girls her age were lounging on the beach, hanging out at the movies, or attending dances. She did not have anyone to share her excitement with, nor did she have someone to whom she could voice her fears.

With a weak smile, Bailey stood, grabbed her glass, and started towards the kitchen. To add to the pretense that she was getting more iced tea, she offered to refill Nonna's glass.

Downstairs, she stopped at the entrance of the kitchen, and mentally cursed her failure to verify Eleanor's whereabouts before leaving the living room. For two hours she had managed to avoid the woman, who had strutted into the house, wearing a black halter dress with a narrow skirt that was more suited for a cocktail party than a baby shower.

As if she sensed someone was watching her, Eleanor glanced over her shoulder at Bailey. The spatula she had been using to scoop a wedge of lasagna from a ceramic pan slid from her grip. It bounced off the table, splattering sauce over the floral centerpiece before it dropped to the floor.

"Shit." Eleanor stomped her black, two-inch heel.

The expletive reached beyond the confines of the kitchen to the back yard where the children were playing hide-and-seek. Norma popped up from behind a bench and craned her neck to see who uttered the curse, while Julia stopped her count at seven and emitted a drawn out, "Ooooh."

Eleanor spun around to the children and muttered a second expletive.

Celeste stepped into the doorway. Her frown suggested the milder word did not redeem the other woman in her eyes. But then again, she had been cross with her cousin-in-law since learning the role Eleanor played in Norma's expulsion.

Bailey had not intended to unburden her problems on anyone. The day was supposed to be a celebration for Georgia and the baby, and she had no plans on dampening the mood. Yet when Julia and Norma hugged like two people who had not seen each other in years, Celeste joked about Georgia and herself behaving in a similar fashion when they were younger. When Bailey failed to crack a smile at the memory, the other woman had insisted she reveal all.

Celeste reached behind her and closed the door leading to the back yard. Seconds later, Julia resumed her count, and feet scrambled to find new hiding places.

"From the sounds of it, they kept the wrong mother at the school," she muttered while grabbing a dishcloth.

"Here, let me." Eleanor reached for the rag.

"You've done enough," Celeste told her, sidestepping the other woman.

With a sigh, Eleanor set her plate on the table, squeezed by Bailey, and headed back upstairs.

Deciding they needed to call a truce for the children's sake, Bailey placed the glasses she carried from the living room into the sink and followed the woman. She reached the top step to the parlor level as Eleanor slipped out the front door.

"For eight years I wondered how you did it," Eleanor said without glancing behind her when the door opened. "When we first met, I was more educated than you. I had more money. And I came from the right family. Yet I could never wrap Matteo around my finger like you. The other night he backed down from a fight 'cause you told him to stop."

Bailey sat on the step next to the woman and listened.

"It was about two years into my marriage when I came to terms with the fact that there was only one woman for him, and it wasn't me. It was then that I wanted to make his life miserable, and it didn't matter who I used to do it."

Bailey felt for Eleanor. It had to be tough to want

someone as much as she did but to not be wanted in return. That still did not excuse the woman's behavior.

The problem was between Matteo and Eleanor and herself. There had been no reason to put the children in the middle.

"Did hurting my baby make you feel better?" Bailey asked.

Eleanor turned to her. "Honestly…" She shook her head. "No." She faced forward again. "It didn't change anything. Matteo still worships the ground you walk on, and I'm barely tolerated by his family."

At least the woman did not get pleasure from her schemes.

"I hope you don't get the wrong idea," Eleanor said. "Just 'cause I'm talking to you doesn't make us friends."

Bailey hmphed. "Any chances of us becoming friends ended when you went after my baby." She could never forgive Eleanor for her role in Norma's expulsion. "I just want to know I'll be able to visit my cousin without worrying about a knife in my back."

Eleanor hesitated a second before she nodded. Satisfied, Bailey stood and headed back inside. She returned to the kitchen, where Celeste was wrapping up an untouched pan of lasagna.

Bailey headed towards the sink as one of Matteo's nephews rushed in from the back yard. He grabbed a cannoli from a tray on the counter before dashing back outside, leaving the door wide open.

"You made more than enough food." Bailey turned on the faucet and grabbed the dishcloth.

"This one's for Papa and Nicky," Celeste replied. "I didn't want to hear them complain that we didn't save them any."

"Why don't you tell Nick to make his own?" According to Georgia, the man was an outstanding cook.

"He'd still whine." Celeste sucked her teeth. "The big baby."

Bailey chuckled. Nicholas and Celeste constantly teased each other, yet there was no question that they cared for each other. And, like Celeste's husband had learned the hard way, no one messed with one of them without suffering consequences from the other.

Unfortunately, Bailey's relationship with her brother did not come close. Though they lived together, she wasn't sure Lincoln would be there for her in times of trouble.

"Did you and Eleanor make peace?" Celeste asked.

"If you're asking if we'll refrain from displays of hair-pulling and eye-scratching, then yes. However, don't expect us to meet for brunch at the Russian Tea Room."

"I wish she had shown that maturity earlier this week."

"You and me both." Bailey sighed.

Celeste placed the pan in the refrigerator. "Have you decided what you're gonna do with Norma while you're at work?"

Bailey shook her head. She had asked Mrs. Roberts. Unfortunately, the woman was leaving to visit friends down south for two weeks.

She did not want to bring Norma to work with her. The girl should be in a classroom, filling her mind with knowledge, not hanging out in a diner, being seduced by shiny coins.

"Listen, you've had a rough week. Why don't you take the night off. Norma can stay here, and I'll bring her home in the morning."

"I'm not sure—" Celeste was good with Norma, but she did not want to burden the woman with more of a reminder of her loss. The baby shower had to be tough enough on her.

"It's not a problem. Julia and several other cousins are also spending the night."

"Please, Miss Collins?" Julia said, skipping into the kitchen. Norma stood in the doorway, her eyes silently pleading with Bailey to agree.

Bailey smiled. She could not say no with all of them ganging up on her. "Fine. She can sleep over."

Squealing, the girls raced back into the yard.

"Now that's settled, what do you plan to do with your night off?" Celeste asked.

Bailey shrugged. A week ago, she would have already made plans with Kyle.

"How about a movie?" Celeste reached for a newspaper sitting on top of a cabinet next to the table.

Bailey was open to the idea. Though most people in the theater would be part of a couple, there was no rule saying she could not go out by herself. And a good comedy could temporarily take her mind off conniving ex-wives and cheating men.

After scanning the newspaper for the latest movies, Bailey said goodnight to Norma, whose lips barely brushed her cheek before she ran off to play hopscotch with Julia. Bailey took the bus downtown and enjoyed a double feature.

Hours later, she strolled towards her building, munching on the remains of her popcorn and contemplating a bubble bath from the gift set Georgia had given her for her birthday several weeks earlier.

Between working on her final papers, studying for her exams, and her job at the diner, she had not yet had the opportunity to enjoy that present.

In the distance, a clock counted to nine. Children scampered towards their respective apartments to get ready for bed so they could rise early for Sunday School. Across the street, the blonde flirt skipped down the steps from her house to a waiting car. A tall, slender man who worked in the grocery store held the passenger side door open for her.

The woman gave her date a quick kiss before she folded herself into the vehicle. She did not appear broken up by Kyle's insistence that she had only been a diversion.

The car drove off, and the street grew quiet. The lull would only last until the next group of adventurers headed out in search of a party.

Bailey stepped into the front yard, then huffed at her inability to see her keys in the dark void of her purse. Once again, Lincoln had ignored the note asking him to replace the burnt-out bulb over the door. Why did she bother to waste her time? It would have been simpler for her to perform the chore herself than to fuss at him to do his share to make their home livable.

She wondered whether his lack of interest in the upkeep of the apartment was a result of her referring to it as "her place," instead of "their place." If he had something to call his own, would he be more inclined to care for it?

Too lazy to step back to the curb, Bailey rummaged blindly through her purse until her fingers grazed the edge of the key. She inserted it in the lock. The cylinder clicked, and a shadow moved.

"What the—" A large, callous hand clamped over her mouth, suppressing the scream. Her heart raced and her body shook. She was supposed to be safe in her home, not accosted by a faceless figure.

Bailey was shoved into the apartment. A shoe smacked the door. The barrier closed, shielding the assault from potential saviors.

Bailey kicked back as the intruder attempted to pin her in place. Her right shoe flew off and landed down the hall with a thud. Her left heel sank into soft flesh.

Her attacker cursed. He spun her around and slammed her back against the wall. With his hand around her neck, he held her up until the tips of her toes only grazed the floor.

The headlight from a passing car illuminated the scowl on the dark face. A jagged scar ran from his missing left earlobe to his Adam's apple.

"Where's Lincoln?" he asked, tightening his grip on her throat.

"I don't know," she gasped as her short nails clawed at his arm.

"He owes me money."

"I don't know anything about it."

"Shit costs money. He can't think he'll take people's shit and not pay."

"I don't get involved in his affairs."

"You're involved now." He pulled her forward, then slammed her head back. "You tell him he either pays up or else."

Bailey shuddered at the "or else." If he didn't get the money from Lincoln, would he, like so many other people in her life, make someone else pay for the sins of another?

"He's got one week to cough up the dough," the man added.

His words sounded far off. It was getting harder for her to focus.

Bailey did not want to pass out with him in her apartment. There was no telling what he would do to an unconscious woman.

She reached forward and dug her nails into his face. The skin tore. Blood covered the tips of her fingers.

With a scream, he released her and touched his face.

Bailey relished her ability to take a deep breath. Her prayer of thanks lasted until the fist connected with her face. Her head snapped to the side. She held her arms up to protect her face, leaving her midsection exposed.

A fist rammed into her stomach. She doubled over and slid to the floor. The only pain that came close to what she felt was contractions. But, unlike labor pains, once the ache subsided, she would not be handed a beautiful child.

"One week." The *thunk* of his hard soles against the wood followed his reminder. A horn bleeped and a driver called out to a buddy down the block. The friend's reply was cut off as the intruder closed the door behind him.

Clutching her stomach, Bailey tried to push up. Her shaky legs refused to support her, and she fell back against the wall.

Tears rolled down her cheeks. Thank heavens Celeste had offered to keep Norma for the night. No one would harm her baby at the Santiano house.

****

The jiggled doorknob broke Bailey's trance. She sat up and listened to the expletive muttered as a key slipped into the lock. The deadbolt turned and the door opened.

"Why the hell is the door locked?" Lincoln stepped into the apartment and tripped over a bag.

Bailey felt a slight sense of satisfaction when he collided with the same wall she had been slammed against hours earlier.

"What's this doing here?" her brother asked, kicking the bag to the side.

Bailey pushed up from the sofa. "Give me your key. Get your shit. And get the fuck out of here."

"What the hell's gotten into you?" he asked, closing the door.

"You're selling drugs."

"Where'd you hear that—"

"Don't lie to me, Lincoln." She pointed to her face. "You had a visitor."

His eyes widened as he took in her half-closed eye. "What happened?"

"Your supplier shoved his way in when I got home. He wanted to know where you were."

"What did you tell him?"

"That I didn't have the least idea where you were."

Lincoln dropped his keys into his jacket pocket. "If that's the case, he won't be back." He slipped the jacket off and tossed it towards the sofa.

Bailey caught the clothing, fished the keys out of the pocket, and tossed it back to him. "I said get the fuck out of here."

"Why?" He caught the jacket. "He's gone and no one was hurt."

"You don't consider a black eye hurt?"

"It'll heal."

"You're un-fucking-believable." She tossed her hands in the air. "What if Norma had been here? My baby could've been hurt." She stepped forward and smacked the back of his head. "I wish I could knock the sense into you."

"Hey!" He jumped back, his hands protectively raised in front of his face. "Don't you be hittin' me."

"Or what? You're gonna put me in a headlock and drag me around the room while I beg you to let me go?" She shook her head. "Not today." She took another step forward at him. "We're no longer children. I'll fight back, and I'll be damned if I don't win."

"Okay, I'm sorry. I'm sorry."

"Yes, you are sorry. Now get the fuck outta here."

"And where do you expect me to go?"

"I don't care." Bailey marched to the door, opened it, and tossed a bag out of the apartment. "And I don't wanna know."

She grabbed a second bag, but Lincoln caught it before it joined the first. "Have you lost your mind?"

"No. In fact, this is the first time I'm thinking clearly." She pushed the bag into his chest. "Now, get out."

"Fine." He stepped around her. "Turn your back on family." He picked up the last bag. "I'm the only one willing to have anything to do with you."

"Maybe I'll be better off on my own."

Lincoln stepped back and tripped over the bag Bailey had already tossed out. A day ago, she would have been at her brother's side, fussing over him, checking if he was all right and offering to fix him a plate of food. But the thought of the danger he had put her and her daughter in hardened her heart. She slammed the door and engaged the lock.

Bailey shuffled to her room, crawled onto the bed,

and hugged her pillow. Her tears dampened the cotton case as her brother struggled to gather his belongings outside.

When all was silent, she sat in the dark and seethed at this latest obstacle in her life.

Chapter Fourteen

"I hope you don't expect me to believe that bull you're spewing?" Celeste asked, after Norma closed the door behind her.

Bailey had not expected her daughter or Celeste to believe she'd walked into a wall. She simply hoped Celeste would have followed Norma's example and dropped the subject. However, the woman's glare said she was not going to leave until she got a believable explanation for Bailey's black eye and the bruises on her neck.

Having gotten rid of one squatter, Bailey was not ready to acquire a new house guest. She perched on the edge of the sofa and confessed, "Lincoln's selling drugs."

"He's what?" Celeste dropped into the armchair.

"He's selling…and possibly doing drugs." She recounted her encounter with the man the previous evening.

"What was he thinking?" Celeste asked.

"I didn't ask for an explanation." Bailey's fingers curled into a tight fist. "I was so pissed I could've torn him apart with my bare hands."

"Do you know where he went?"

Bailey's head moved from side to side. She did not know, and she did not care. For the first time, she had no desire to have any contact with her brother.

"You need to tell Nicky," Celeste said.

That was the last thing Bailey needed to do. While Lincoln did not lay a finger on her, his actions were the reason she did not feel safe in her own home for the first time in six years. As far as the Santianos were concerned, anything less than a cast on one of his limbs was not a good enough punishment.

Bailey agreed Lincoln needed to face the consequences of his actions, which was why he no longer resided under her roof. But she did not want him hurt. No matter what, he was her brother.

"Leave Nicholas out of this," Bailey said, hoping an eviction would force Lincoln to get clean.

"But—"

"No, he's gone, and I want to move on."

Celeste patted her hands, but her shoulders slumped in defeat.

Bailey knew the other woman disagreed with her choice, but she could not allow them to harm Lincoln. Her brother deserved the same second chance she had given Matteo. She only hoped he took advantage of the gift she gave him.

****

Matteo tripped over the toolbox as he raced from the bathroom to the bedroom to answer the telephone. His knee hit the metal bed frame. The pain radiating from the joint made his eyes cross.

"*Dannazione*! He muttered the mild expletive as he snatched the headset off the base and pressed it against his ear.

"Bailey needs your help," Celeste announced before he uttered a greeting.

"What happened?" he asked, ignoring the throbbing

in his knee. It had to be serious for his cousin to call him.

Matteo calmly listened to her account of her conversation with Bailey, then agreed to check on his friend. When he heard the click on the other end of the phone, the calm he had managed to maintain broke. He slammed the headset onto the base and shouted, "*Merda*!"

Moving slower than he wanted, Matteo limped out of the building to the corner. He pulled his wallet from his pocket and shoved a five into the hand of the father who had opened the rear cab door for his wife and daughter. He slipped into the vehicle and barked Bailey's address to the driver.

"You don't expect me to go to that neighborhood?" the driver asked.

"You'll go wherever the fuck I tell you," Matteo replied.

He ignored the sanctimonious gasp from the woman who had stepped back onto the sidewalk. Two nights earlier she'd hurled a litany of curses at her husband when she confronted him outside their apartment building about money missing from their bank account thanks to his gambling habit.

Matteo tossed another five into the front seat, certain the nickel would make the man temporarily get over his aversion to driving through a neighborhood in which *he* would be the minority. The driver stared at the money for two seconds before pulling away from the curb.

Unable to relax, Matteo leaned forward and gripped the back of the front seat. It was all his fault. After Norma's expulsion, he had not wanted to burden Bailey's mind with his concerns about Lincoln. Had he spoken up sooner, maybe they could have figured out how bad things were before she had been attacked.

The driver slowed down, then stopped at a yellow light. Matteo slammed his palm on the front seat and cursed.

The man glanced at him through the rearview mirror. His scowl failed to calm his passenger.

Matteo glared back. The driver needed to consider himself lucky that he did not insist on driving, a move not for the faint of heart. His impatience would have had him ignoring every rule of the road to get to Bailey in record time.

What had the woman been thinking? Why didn't she leave the apartment? Why hadn't she called him? And, most importantly, who was he going to introduce to their Maker for laying hands on her?

Twenty minutes after he convinced the driver to take the fare, the taxicab pulled up in front of Bailey's apartment. She sat on the stoop, flipping through a catalog.

When she glanced up, the evidence of her attack sent his blood pressure through the roof.

****

"Have you lost your ever-lovin' mind?" Matteo bellowed, his red face growing darker with each passing second.

Bailey had to give it to him. Despite the murderous look in his eyes when he stepped from the cab, he had remained calm long enough to hand Norma and her two friends a dollar each and send them to the store before he marched into the apartment and exploded.

"Since when are you and Celeste on speaking terms?"

"Don't change the subject." His face scrunched in

rage.

Though Bailey had never seen him that angry, she had no fear…at least for her own safety.

"I didn't want to tell you 'cause I knew you'd act like this," she replied.

"Like what?" Matteo tossed his hands up. "Someone concerned for your wellbeing?"

"A crazed madman."

"How do you expect me to act after someone smacked you around?"

"It wasn't like that."

"Your bruises tell a different story."

Bailey did not flinch when he reached towards her. He cupped the back of her neck, and his thumb gently caressed her jawline.

"I'm gonna knock the sense into Lincoln's thick skull."

Translation, *Lincoln was going to visit the great beyond.*

Bailey pulled away from him. "Leave my brother alone."

"What?"

"I said—"

"Are you kidding me?"

"Lincoln deserves a second chance. Like the one I gave you."

He released a long sigh. Bailey had expected an argument. Instead he asked, "Who did this?"

"He didn't say."

"Bailey—"

"We didn't exchange names and pleasantries before he pushed his way in."

Matteo sighed. "What did he look like?"

Bailey described the face etched in her mind. It would be a long time—if ever—before his image faded from her memory.

"Where's your brother?" Matteo asked.

"I don't know. He took his bags and left this morning."

Matteo's hand dropped to her shoulder. He pulled her to his chest and held her tight. She inhaled the cigarette smoke in his clothes, and his aftershave, and for the first time since the attack, she felt safe.

"You're moving," Matteo said.

"No, I'm not," Bailey replied.

"I didn't ask you."

"I know you didn't, but either way, I'm not moving."

This was her apartment, and some dealer was not going to run her out of it. She would buy new locks for the doors, change the lightbulb on the outside of the building, and make a habit of being more aware of her surroundings. She would do whatever it took to feel safe again—except move.

"You kicked your brother out, so everything's fine?" Matteo asked.

"Yes," she mumbled into his chest.

"Don't be so naive." He grasped her shoulders and pulled back from her. "It's not that simple. That man's not gonna leave you alone 'til he finds your brother or gets his money."

She pushed his hands away. "I'm not packing *my* bags or leaving *my* house."

"So what do you plan to do? Stay here and wait for him to return? I'm sure he's gonna enjoy knocking you around again. Or maybe he'll get his kicks from slamming Norma into a wall."

****

Bailey's face twisted in horror. Matteo felt awful, but he had no choice but to be blunt with her.

He understood her attachment to the apartment. Finding the place had been the first step she had taken to show everyone—including herself—that she could not only make it on her own but achieve a goal she set her mind to. Now, thanks to her brother, she was about to lose what she had worked so hard to hold on to.

He wanted to sleep on her sofa until they were certain her attacker would not return, but that would lead to tongues wagging. Neither Norma nor Bailey needed to deal with the malicious gossip that would follow them long after he returned home.

His apartment was too small for the three of them. There was only one full-size bed in the space that was barely big enough for one man to move about without running into things.

"Celeste wants Norma and you to stay with her," he announced.

"I can't put her out," Bailey said. "And I won't impose on Georgia. She'll have enough to deal with once the baby arrives. She wouldn't need the extra company disrupting her household."

"You won't be putting Celeste out. No one's using Nicholas's old bedroom, and Norma can sleep in the playroom."

"What will Mr. Santiano have to say?"

"My uncle will probably scold you for not returning last night."

The new living arrangement would prevent him from visiting, but her safety was more important than his

177

wants.

Bailey hesitated another minute before nodding her head. "Fine. I just need to pack a few things."

"Where's your suitcase?"

She pointed to the closet. Matteo opened the door and spotted the baby blue bag he had bought her years ago.

"You kept this," he said, pulling the bag from the shelf.

She shrugged.

Despite the gesture, Matteo smiled. It may not seem like a big deal to her, but it meant a lot to him that she would cherish something as simple as a bag.

Bailey took the suitcase. "Get Norma for me?"

Matteo stepped outside, where the girl and her friends were sitting on the stoop, sorting through three piles of sweets. Too late, he realized he should not have given each girl a dollar; one buck would have been enough for the three of them. Now the girls would later suffer for his impulsiveness.

"Norma, your mother wants you," he called to the girl.

She swept her loot into a small brown paper bag, then bounced off the steps to his side.

"If you eat all that at once, you'll get a stomachache."

"I know that." The "duh" in her tone would have made him feel silly for stating the obvious had her cheeks not been bulging from the gumdrops she had stuffed into her mouth.

By the time they stepped inside, Bailey had five complete outfits spread out on the bed. She glanced at the bag in the girl's fist and rolled her eyes.

"Norma, we're going to stay with Cousin Celeste for a couple of days," she announced.

"Why?" The girl asked.

"I had a little trouble last night. Matteo thinks it would be better if we stay with her," she replied, offering enough to inform the girl without worrying her.

"Can I take Penelope?"

Bailey held out her hand. "Go get what you need."

The girl passed the bag of candy to her mother and ran past the bed to the toy bin at the far end of the kitchen.

"What do you need me to do?" Matteo asked.

"I need you to promise you won't go after Lincoln," Bailey said, turning to the dresser.

Matteo pursed his lips together. He had no desire to make such a promise because then he would be bound to keep his word instead of beating the mess out of her brother.

Bailey tossed a pair of white pajamas with multicolored balloons onto the bed. She crossed her arms over her chest. Her eyes narrowed as she silently challenged him not to abide by her wish.

As tempting as it was to hear what she could come up with to convince him to give his word, he did not want to argue with her. He wanted to get her packed and out of the apartment so he could deal with the man who had dared to lay hands on her in an unloving manner.

"Fine, I won't go after Lincoln…this time. But if anything else happens…"

"We'll hope nothing else happens."

Just like he did not believe in purple fairies granting wishes, he did not believe her brother would get clean anytime soon. He personally understood the power of drugs. They promised to solve problems while blinding users to the additional ones they created. They could take down anyone, regardless of the user's age, gender, or socioeconomic background.

Matteo's instinct told him Bailey's attack would not inspire her brother to get clean. It was going to take more before the man said enough was enough and sought help. Matteo was afraid to know how much more.

Her eyes shone bright with determination. He had seen the same spark when she announced she was going to college. But, unlike her previous goal, getting Lincoln straight was out of her control.

Instead of vocalizing his concerns, Matteo kissed her forehead. It was the one time he prayed he was wrong.

****

"Some help, please," Norma called out from behind the mountain of toys in her arms.

"What do you have there?" Bailey asked, taking a stuffed rabbit and bear from the top of the stack.

Norma dropped her burden on the bed. "You told me to get what I need."

"You don't need all of this."

"Yes, I do." The girl pulled the colored rag doll from under her arm. "Penelope needs a change of clothes, her bottle, her blankie and her book."

"You don't need these." Bailey waved the stuffed animals in the air.

"She's never been away from home. She might get scared."

"There's nothing for her to be scared of. I'll be there, as well as Celeste, Mr. Santiano, and Nonna."

"What about Mr. Matteo?"

"No, he won't be able to come with us."

Disappointment weighed on Bailey. Since the afternoon she went into labor, he had been there, comforting her with his words and presence whenever she was afraid or overwhelmed.

"Why?" Norma asked.

"I have to work," Matteo replied.

Bailey would not question the work he had to do. He had given his word that he would leave Lincoln alone. Whatever else he needed to do was his business.

A car screeched to a halt in front of the house. Bailey raised an eyebrow at Matteo, then sighed at his shrug. Celeste had continued spreading the word about the encounter after speaking to him.

Hoping to avoid what would be the equivalent of the next world war in her apartment, Bailey raced out of the room. She made it to the living room entrance as the door flew open and Nicholas rushed in.

He stopped short and gaped at her. His right hand cupped her chin and turned her head to get a better look at the bruises on the side of her face.

"Did he—?"

"No," Bailey replied. "He didn't touch me."

Nicholas took a deep breath, then proved he not only looked like his cousin but possessed the same personality. "Why the hell didn't you call us?" he bellowed.

To be honest, she was not sure where she stood with the rest of the Santiano clan. Yes, she attended cookouts, birthdays and weddings, but she always figured the invitations were due to her relationship with Georgia. She was never under the illusion the protection afforded her cousin was extended to her.

"Where's your brother?" Nicholas asked without

waiting for the answer to his previous question.

"I don't know," she replied.

"Bailey—"

"Like I told Matteo, he took his bags and left this morning."

"Matteo?" He peered over her head. "Did you have anything to do with this? *Ti uccidero*!"

Nicholas took a step forward. Bailey jumped in front of him and pressed her hands against his chest.

"Matteo had nothing to do with this," she snapped at Nicholas's insistence on ending Matteo's existence on the planet. "You lay a hand on him, and I won't go anywhere with you. *Giuro che sono serio*," she added to emphasize her seriousness.

Nicholas's nostrils flared, reminding Bailey of a bull preparing to charge. She'd seen one in a movie once and never forgotten it. Instead of charging, Nicholas inhaled deeply and stepped back.

Matteo simply cocked an eyebrow. "When did you start understanding Italian?"

"It's impossible to be around y'all and not pick up a word or two," Bailey said.

Nicholas shook his head. "We can discuss the languages you can understand another time. Georgia's anxious to see you."

"Why didn't she come?" Bailey asked.

"Didn't know if your attack—"

Bailey cleared her throat and jerked her head in the direction of the bedroom, where Norma was adding more toys to the pile on the bed.

"—your visitor was still hanging around," Nicholas said. "Are you about ready?"

"I need a few more minutes," Bailey replied.

"I need to speak to you." Matteo's calm tone worried her more than Nicholas's bellow. She suspected they were about to make decisions about her life with no regard to her feelings about the matter.

Bailey had been the sole decision-maker for her affairs since moving from her uncle's apartment six years earlier. She could not relinquish control simply because two men needed to see who could puff his chest out more.

"There's nothing you have to say to him," she said.

"I agree," Nicholas replied, his hands tightening into fists by his side.

Matteo stepped next to Bailey's side. "A word." He jerked his head at the door.

Bailey was tempted to follow them. They needed to remember it was her life. They could not make plans without her.

At the same time, she needed to return to the bedroom and explain to Norma that they could not take the entire contents of her toy chest.

After a second, she decided to let them believe they were in control. If they made any decisions she disagreed with, she had no problem putting her foot down and telling them "no."

Nicholas and Matteo stepped outside and closed the door. When the sound of fists smacking flesh did not interrupt the peace in the neighborhood, she returned to the bedroom to pack a week's worth of clothes for Norma, three outfits for herself, and seven dresses for the doll.

Bailey emerged from the apartment with the suitcase in one hand and her handbag draped over the other arm. Matteo stepped into the yard, took the luggage and lifted it up and down, testing the weight.

"This is all you're taking?"

"I can get whatever I need when I check the mail," she replied, locking the door.

"I prefer you let me do it. I can drop it off at the diner."

"I agree with him," Nicholas said.

The little energy left after a fitful night's sleep was slowly draining. She still had to listen to Georgia, Mr. Santiano, and Nonna fuss at her for not reaching out to them. Therefore, she could only offer Matteo, "We'll talk about it later."

He carried the suitcase to the car and placed it in the back seat.

"I need you to sit in the back today," she told Norma, who cradled her doll while waiting to climb into the vehicle.

As her daughter scrambled into the car, Matteo took Bailey's hand. "Get some rest, Shorty. If you need anything—"

"Do you mind stopping by the library tomorrow and telling them I'm unable to make reading time?"

He nodded. "Anything else?"

"Not right now."

Matteo tugged on the arm. She stepped forward until she felt his heartbeat against her chest. He enclosed his arms around her. The embrace was meant to comfort her and reassure her everything would be all right. And though he would not be able to visit while she was staying with his relatives, she believed his unspoken promise.

Chapter Fifteen

Matteo felt useless watching Bailey ride off with his cousin. Since the day he found her in labor—alone and scared—he had protected, comforted, and reassured her. But thanks to his past sins, he had to relinquish her protection to Nicholas.

His cousin would undoubtedly make sure Bailey was safe. But Matteo did not want to turn over the job to anyone else. He wanted to watch over Bailey, hold her tight, and get as much comfort from the embrace as he gave her.

Knowing none of his wants would be fulfilled that day, Matteo walked home. The exercise was supposed to help defuse his anger at Bailey's attack and his inability to be there for her. All it did was give him more time to think about her situation, and the more he thought, the angrier he got.

Needing time to himself to stew, Matteo headed to the basement when he arrived home. Unfortunately, the universe had not conveyed his desire to be alone to Liam.

"Where were you?" the teen asked, when Matteo opened the door to his apartment.

Since no one had inquired about his whereabouts since he was sixteen, Matteo peered over his shoulder, looking for the person the question had been directed to. Seeing no in the empty hall behind him, he turned back and cocked an eyebrow at the young man sitting at his table.

"Out minding my own business," he answered, closing the door. "There's a reason you're here?"

"Yeah." Liam pointed to his face. "How do I get rid of a shiner?"

The boy's black eye reminded Matteo of Bailey's bruise. He silently cursed himself for being a screw-up. Had he not messed up, he'd be with the woman instead of dealing with a boy who had lately become a magnet for trouble.

"If you're into makeup, try powder, otherwise leave it alone and it'll fade in time," Matteo replied.

"I was afraid of that." The boy slumped in the chair.

Having never been interested in theater, Matteo was unimpressed by Liam's dramatics. The kid needed to take lessons from Eleanor on getting to the point. The woman was able to rattle off three grievances before Matteo had both feet over the threshold when he would return home from work in the evenings.

A minute passed before he became exasperated enough to ask, "You gonna tell me what happened, or do you expect me to guess?"

"I got into a fight."

Matteo did not want to push the boy away, yet his patience was running thin. He was seconds away from grabbing the boy by the shoulders and shaking the story from him.

He closed his eyes, took a deep breath and began counting in Italian. "*Dieci. Nove. Otto…*"

"Whatcha doin'?" Liam asked.

Matteo stopped his count at four and opened his eyes. "Trying to keep from giving you another black eye," he replied, feeling no calmer than he had before starting the exercise recommended at the support group he attended to help him stay clean. "It's not working."

The boy swallowed hard. He sat back and blurted out, "I was hanging with the guys last night and they decided to play T-and-A with this girl…"

"And she belted you?" Disappointment weighed on Matteo. After their discussion the previous Sunday, he'd thought the boy would have more respect for women.

"No, my friend…well, I guess he's no longer my friend…he did."

Confused, Matteo pulled out the other chair and sat across from the boy. "What happened?"

His disappointment switched to pride as Liam explained how he first tried to talk the other guys out of the assault, then got into a fight with the instigator when the other boy refused to back down.

"Grandma's gonna lose it when she sees my eye." Liam sighed.

"How'd you hide it from her?" Matteo asked.

"She was already in bed when I got in last night. This morning, I told her I didn't feel well, and then I laid on my side until she left for church. If she doesn't lose her sight before she gets home, I'm done."

The boy's antics reminded Matteo of the schemes Nicholas and he had tried to pull to avoid a scolding from the peace-loving matriarch of the Santiano family, who did not approve when they got into altercations. However, if Mrs. Murphy was like his grandmother, she would not reprimand him for helping another.

"Your grandmother will be proud of you."

"What…why…how…" Liam stuttered.

"You defended a girl. That was honorable. I'm proud of you."

A smile spread across Liam's face. The eye that was not swollen shut brightened with the satisfaction that came from a mentor's approval.

Matteo also felt a sense of pride. His opinion mattered to someone. It had been a hard road from fuck-up to mentor. He just wished his family could see how far he had come.

****

"You should be in bed," Celeste announced, stepping into the kitchen lit only by the dim light from the hall.

Bailey could not argue with her, considering it had been thirty-six hours since she had gotten any sleep. The afternoon had been spent answering questions by the endless number of people intent on interrogating her about the previous night's events as well as any knowledge she had of Lincoln's dealings.

When she finally had a moment to herself, too many thoughts played in her mind for her to get any rest. Not only did she relive the attack every time she closed her eyes, but she also worried about the what-ifs. What if the man found Lincoln? What if he didn't and returned to her home? Or, more importantly, what if he followed her back to the Santianos' home?

Of course, the last question should not have concerned her. If he was foolish enough to show up at her refuge, he would be dealt with swiftly and, most likely, painfully.

Instead of replying, Bailey pushed the cookie jar she had been pinching from into the center of the table. The other woman set down a bottle of whiskey and two glasses.

Bailey eyed the bottle before raising her head and

cocking an eyebrow.

"It's from Daddy's supply." Celeste uncorked the bottle and poured each of them a healthy serving.

Bailey raised her glass to her, then swallowed a mouthful of the amber liquid. The alcohol scorched her throat, her eyes watered, and her sinuses cleared.

"This tastes like the stash Uncle James keeps under his kitchen sink," Bailey gasped between coughs.

Celeste shrugged a shoulder. "I didn't say where Daddy got this from," she replied, sliding into the chair catty-corner to Bailey.

"A little warning would be appreciated next time," Bailey said as she held out her glass.

Celeste refilled both their glasses, then set the bottle next to the cookie jar.

Bailey sighed. "Y'all must think I'm foolish for not knowing Lincoln was using." In hindsight, he had been exhibiting the same signs Matteo had when he was on drugs, the moodiness and outbursts, the risky behavior, and the change in his appearance.

When Lincoln first moved in with her, he would've never walked around the house in dingy drawers and an undershirt. He always had to look sharp. His clothes were clean and pressed, and he was washed, with slick waves in his hair.

"You're not foolish," Celeste said. "You loved him too much to believe he'd mess with that stuff,"

Honestly, Bailey wasn't sure whether it was love or her desire to have some connection to her family. Either way, her decision to overlook what was right before her eyes resulted in her being forced from her home.

"I'm curious," Celeste said as she settled back in her chair.

"About?" Bailey asked.

"Why Matteo?"

The woman did not need to say more than those two words for Bailey to understand her concern. Matteo was a junkie who lied and stole from his family. He was only breathing because he never laid hands on a woman, unlike Celeste's husband.

Bailey had wanted to abide by the code when he walked into the diner six months after his family disowned him. Yet, when she looked at him, she did not see a strung-out man, desperate for his next fix. Instead, when she gazed into his soft blue eyes, she had been reminded of the man who had gone out of his way to assist a frightened girl who was not prepared to deal with the consequences of the grown-up game she had played nine months earlier.

"Whenever I felt alone, Matteo was there, letting me know I didn't have to face things by myself," Bailey replied, reliving the memories of each moment he had been there for her. "When I announced I was going back to school, Uncle James asked how I planned to do so with a child. Matteo, on the other hand, told me to go for it." He had kissed her forehead before he made the statement, as if he was transferring some of his strength to her.

The doubt in Celeste's eyes said forgiveness would be harder for her, which led Bailey to wonder, "Why'd you call Matteo after you left my house?"

Celeste knocked back the rest of her drink and poured another before she replied, "I figured if anyone could convince you to go somewhere safe, it would be him."

Bailey appreciated the woman's honesty and felt it

would only be right for her to confess, "I'm surprised you opened your home to me."

"Why wouldn't I?" Celeste asked.

"You're Georgia's friend. I never expected the benefits she got from being associated with your family to extend to me."

"I'm sorry Georgia and I used to exclude you when we were younger."

They had never invited Bailey to the beach or to hang out with them at a diner. But it was not like she expected them to want a pregnant girl, and then later a baby, tagging along. She had let Norma's father between her legs, and it was she, not anyone else, who had to face the consequences of her actions.

"However, the Santianos are big on family," Celeste continued. "When Mr. Collins took you in, you became a part of the family."

And as a part of the family, Bailey was expected to follow the same codes as everyone else. But no matter how much they helped her, she could not walk away from Matteo.

Chapter Sixteen

A smile tugged on the corners of Bailey's lips as she admired the yellow rose lying on top of the envelopes on the counter in front of Matteo. His little gestures had always gone a long way in turning a stressful day around.

"How you doing, Shorty?" He gently brushed his fingertips over the bruise that was still visible despite the thick layer of powder she had applied before leaving for work. It was one time she was grateful for the customers' lack of attention to her. Their inattentiveness limited the number of questioning glances directed at her.

"Tired," she confessed as the bell rang, signaling the departure of the last diner for the day.

"Can't sleep?"

Bailey nodded, hoping he would not press her for more details. She did not want to admit her concern for Lincoln was partially responsible for her tossing and turning all night.

Matteo glanced around the diner. "Where's Norma?"

"Celeste insisted on watching her. They were supposed to go out today to buy some fabric to make a pouch for all the clues Norma finds."

"Has she found anything?"

"She found an old barrette while digging up the patch of soil in the back yard."

Bailey's heart raced when she recalled the gun she

had found in the living room. She needed to go through every inch of the space to make sure her brother hadn't stashed anything else in the apartment.

"I'm sorry to bring you more bad news, but Norma wasn't the only one searching the apartment. Someone trashed your place last night. None of the windows were broken. They probably picked the front lock."

Or the intruder had been smart enough to get a spare key made in the event she took back the one she had originally given him.

Bailey sighed. "I'll change the locks when I get back."

"Already done." Matteo held up his hand. Two keys hung from a stainless-steel ball chain draped over his forefinger.

A tear slipped over her lower eyelid before she could blink it back. Was there any end to this man's kindness?

"Hey, none of that." He climbed off his stool and stepped behind the counter.

Bailey had not realized she was one kind gesture from crumbling until his arms went around her. The dam broke and she released her pain and anger into his chest.

Everything was going wrong. When she achieved her goals, life was supposed to get better. Yet it felt as if the universe was not satisfied unless it placed more hurdles in her way.

Matteo held her with no complaints about the tears soaking through his shirt. And he did not offer words of comfort but allowed the small circles his hand traced on her back to relay his determination to be there for her.

Bailey cried until there was nothing left inside. Matteo continued to hold her, only pulling back when she released a deep sigh.

"Better?" He pulled back just enough to stare into her eyes.

The tears did not fix her apartment, eliminate the dealer, and get Lincoln clean, yet she felt lighter having released them.

She nodded.

"You're almost ready to go?" He wiped her cheeks with the back of his hand.

"Anita had to leave early." Bailey hiccupped, an annoying aftereffect of crying. "I have to close up."

"What's left for you to do?"

"I have to wash the dishes." She pointed to the table in the center of the room. "Then mop the floor."

He kissed her forehead. "You take care of the floor, and I'll wash the dishes."

"Thank…" She hiccupped. "…you."

"Get a drink of water first." He chuckled.

Bailey poured a drink from the pitcher next to the coffeepot and downed the water in three gulps while Matteo gathered the plates and silverware left behind by the last customer. He carried the dishes into the kitchen as she as poured a second glass.

She was moving the pitcher back to the counter when the bell tinkled.

"Sorry, we're closed," she announced without looking up.

"I know," Lincoln replied.

Startled, she released the pitcher when it was only halfway over the counter. With a curse, she fumbled to catch the container—and spilled the contents onto the floor.

"What are you doing here?" she asked, setting the empty pitcher down.

"I need your help."

His disheveled clothes looked like he had slept in them since Sunday. His eyes were glassy and his hands shook when he swiped at his nose.

Bailey shook her head. He needed more help than she could give.

"You can't turn your back on family," Lincoln insisted.

His definition of family and hers varied. Over the years, she'd learned blood ties did not determine who one's family was but who was there for her in a time of need. The people directly related to her by blood had either turned their backs on her when she needed them most or brought trouble to her door. Her distant relatives had taken her in and people with no ties to her had been there to help protect her from the mess her brother made.

"I can't do anything for you 'til you get clean," Bailey said.

"Come on, I need to pay this guy," Lincoln said. "I promise, once I do, I'll get clean."

A part of Bailey wanted to believe him. Matteo was proof people could get clean. But even if she did want to help... "I don't have the kind of money I suspect you owe him."

"You could ask that man who's always hanging around. His family's loaded." Lincoln sniffed. "What's the use of you hooking up with a white man if you're not getting anything from him?"

"I never asked Matteo for anything," Bailey replied.

"Woman, you're so backwards. They're supposed to pay for the lay." Lincoln snorted. "You givin' it away 'cause you're no good at it? That why your man stepped out on you?"

Bailey raised her hand and swung. Lincoln caught her wrist before her palm connected with his face. He squeezed her arm tight. No doubt she would walk away with another bruise from their encounter.

"Even if I was gonna start asking Matteo for favors, I wouldn't waste any of it on a junkie," Bailey said.

Lincoln leaned his face inches from hers. "You're always sat on your high horse, lookin' down your nose on family." His scowl distorted his features. "Just remember, when he gets tired of you, he's gonna follow the same path Kyle took."

In no mood to listen to anything else her brother had to say, Bailey jerked free of his grasp. Her hand flew to the side and smacked the pitcher. The container crashed to the floor and shattered.

She jumped back. Her foot slipped on the water. She caught hold of the counter before she fell on a jagged piece of glass.

The kitchen door flew open. "Are you okay?" Matteo stopped. His gaze jumped from Bailey to her brother.

Before anyone could react, he introduced his fist to her brother's face.

Lincoln stumbled back into a table, slipped off the edge and onto the floor, the furniture toppling onto him.

****

Matteo stepped forward, determined to take out his frustration on Lincoln's face. He was forced to stop when a hand pulled on his arm.

"Don't hurt him," Bailey begged.

His mouth dropped open, yet he could not get the words out. How could she still protect her brother after he'd laid hands on her? What was it going to take before

196

she allowed the man to suffer the consequences of his actions?

"Go, Lincoln," she yelled.

Demonstrating he had some sense, her brother scrambled to his feet.

The annoying tinkle of the little bell broke Matteo's trance. He snatched his arm from Bailey's grip and took off after her brother.

Lincoln dashed down the block and across the street. A truck's horn bleeped, warning Matteo of the driver's intention of making the light. By the time the vehicle had passed, Bailey's brother had jumped on the bus.

Matteo yelled at the driver to wait. He ceased his chase when the vehicle pulled away from the corner. Muttering a curse, he punched the air.

He was torn between continuing his pursuit to the next bus stop and heading home. Returning to Bailey was not in the equation. If he saw her, he would ask her to choose…her brother or him. Why should he bother sticking his neck out for her if she was going to continue to protect the other man?

It took all of one second for Matteo to make up his mind. With a sigh, he spun around and marched back to the diner. If he could not turn his back on her when it was for her own good, there was no way in hell he would walk away in her time of need.

Bailey had picked up the table and was righting a chair when he walked in.

"If you're going to yell at me, then do me a favor and leave," she said.

Matteo picked up a chair and slammed it down before ignoring her request. "How many chances are you gonna give him?" he yelled.

"I don't know. How many did I give you?"

Matteo's conscience murmured, *Way more than you deserved.*

By the time Eleanor had kicked him out, Matteo's main concern was his next high. His nights were spent in bars and his days sleeping it off. He skipped work more times than he attended. And he only went home to change his clothes and tuck his daughter in bed. But when he showed up at her door with his bags, Bailey let him spend the night on her sofa, then helped him find an apartment the next day. And after the family learned he had been stealing from them and disowned him, she continued to associate with him.

Still, no matter had bad things got, "I never laid a hand on Eleanor. Lincoln shoved you."

"He only grabbed my wrist," Bailey explained. "I slipped when I pulled away."

As much as it pained him, Matteo knew he had to either accept Bailey's devotion to Lincoln or walk away. It was one of the toughest decisions he'd ever had to make. Staying meant watching someone he cared about continually set herself up for disappointment, while walking away meant turning his back on her.

The mental debate lasted less than sixty seconds. Of course he was staying.

Maybe with him around, Lincoln would rethink trying something else. And, if he didn't rethink it, at least there would be someone around to protect her.

"You take care of the dishes, and I'll mop the floor," he said, reassigning the chores.

Bailey released the chair she had been gripping and headed into the kitchen. Matteo stacked the chairs on the table, then swept and mopped the floor. After returning the supplies to the utility closet, he strolled into the kitchen to check if she needed help with anything else.

Faced with an empty room, he started towards the office when he heard a crash in the supply room off the rear of the kitchen.

"Are you okay?" he asked, picking up the can of peaches that rolled across the floor from the storage room.

"I'm fine," Bailey replied.

Matteo stepped around the corner, where she stood in front of a set of metal shelves, rubbing her left shoulder.

"What happened?"

"I must have hit it against the counter when I fell."

He placed the peaches on the shelf next to her head. "Let me see," he said, pulling at the collar of her uniform.

"Wait a minute." Bailey unbuttoned the top until he could push the material aside.

The fading bruise suggested she had initially been injured when the intruder shoved her into her apartment. She must have aggravated the injury during her argument with Lincoln.

Having nothing to treat the bruise, Matteo kissed her shoulder.

Bailey gasped. She shuddered as she leaned back onto him.

Her response was exactly what Matteo had dreamed of more than once over the years. It was music he could listen to over and over again.

His mind warned him against making another move. She was off limits. They should not be friends, much less go to the next level. Before he could remind his feet how to walk away, she turned around and rendered him incapable of reasoning.

Bailey's lips pressed against his and all he could think about was his own need. Right and wrong was pushed aside. He would deal with his conscience after he heard her moan with pleasure and felt her tremble in his arms.

Gripping her by the waist, Matteo moved them until her back was against the wall. "It's All in the Game" played from the radio sitting on the shelf next to the stove. They swayed to the music, their bodies pressed against each other. Though fully clothed, their slow dance took him to the edge.

Matteo pushed up her dress at the same time Bailey reached for his zipper. They pushed aside clothes until they were able to stroke bare flesh.

He shuddered as her hand wrapped around him and slowly moved up and down his length. The rise of the corners of her lips said she approved of what she held.

Believing she should not be the only one appreciating the present company, he slipped a finger inside her. She moaned and writhed against him. Not only was she wet and ready, but she was also eager to accept him.

Not wanting to make her—or him, for that matter—wait any longer, Matteo pulled his wallet from his back pocket. He blindly searched the billfold until he located the foil wrapper.

When Matteo pressed the condom into her free hand, she opened the rubber as he pushed her underwear down her thighs. As his clothes also were lowered, she covered him, protecting them both from another surprise in nine months.

Bailey shimmied until her underwear dropped all the

way to her feet. When she lifted a foot away from the material, he hooked her leg over his arm, and dipped until he was at the right angle to push forward and enter her.

Sighs of contentment filled the air, but there was an urgency to continue. They didn't want to waste time savoring the moment. They would relish the experience another time, when they were also berating themselves for crossing a line that had been clearly drawn.

Bailey held onto Matteo, her head buried in his shoulder as he moved inside her. The slapping of flesh against flesh and their moans drowned out the DJ's chatter on the radio. They had a need more pressing than the newest release from some artist who would be a threat to the heartthrob currently serving overseas.

The intensity grew and Matteo's legs shook. He tried to hold out, not wanting to come without her. But the pressure was too much, and his body took over. He pressed deep inside her and saw stars.

Bailey shuddered beneath him. Her hold tightened and she cried out as she also found relief.

When the shivers faded, he slipped out and lowered her leg. She maintained her grip on him as if afraid of letting him go.

"You're gonna take off now?"

He understood the question and the hint of fear in her voice. Twice they had kissed and twice he had pushed her away. Yet even though he knew walking away would be the smartest move, he could only shake his head to let her know he wasn't going anywhere.

Chapter Seventeen

Matteo could not get used to the dead gaze in Celeste's eyes. He wanted to go a few rounds with her husband—to make the man pay for the pain he'd inflicted on her. But, thanks to his own habit, he would never get the opportunity.

"You gonna continue staring at me, or do you plan to state the purpose of your visit?" Celeste asked, pulling him out of his stupor.

He needed to make things right with the one woman still speaking to him. Though it had only been a gesture, he had told her with a shake of his head that he would not run off. Yet problems with the building had kept him away from the diner for three days. When he finally had a chance to get away, he was told she had not come in.

"Bailey wasn't at work," he replied.

"Georgia went into labor last night. Bailey accompanied Nicholas to the hospital."

Matteo breathed a sigh of relief. On the bus ride to his cousin's house, various scenarios had raced through his mind, and the most disturbing one included Lincoln or his dealer hurting her.

The telephone rang and Celeste mumbled, "Hold on," before she ran back into the house.

Matteo caught the door before it could close in his face. He had not intended to listen to the conversation, but the gasp caught his attention. He crossed the threshold as she dropped the handset on the base and turned back to him. Her face was pale, and for a second he feared she would be sick.

"What's wrong?" he asked.

"Your father had a heart attack," Celeste replied.

Matteo grabbed the banister of the steps leading to the upper floors. A chill coursed through him. "Is he…"

"He's at the hospital. The doctors are working on him now."

Shame and sorrow consumed him. His father could pass on without Matteo ever apologizing for the hurt he'd caused his parent. "I need to borrow your car," Matteo said, releasing the carved baluster.

"You can't go over there," Celeste said.

"He's my father, for Christ sakes. I need to see him."

Doubt flickered in Celeste's eyes. However, it did not matter to him whether she took him or not. He would hail a cab, take the bus—or walk, if he had to.

"Fine, I'll drive you." She slipped past him and called upstairs. "Norma."

The girl ran down from the upper level. "Cousin Celeste, I think I found a clue." She held out her right hand to show off an orange-and-white glass marble.

"That's beautiful, Busy Bee, but we need to go out."

Norma pulled a blue pouch from the front pocket of her peach dress and dropped her discovery inside. "Can I take these?" She held up the doll and book in her other hand.

"I think that would be the best thing." Celeste waved her towards the door. "Come on," she said, grabbing her purse off the end table.

Outside, Norma climbed into the back seat of the blue Studebaker parked in front of the house. Matteo instinctively headed around to the driver's side. He opened the door and Celeste ducked under his arm and into the car.

Her actions reminded him of the changes that had occurred in the past two years. Celeste was no longer a carefree young woman content to sit back and let others do things for her. Once she'd physically recovered from the last beating her husband gave her, she took the steps necessary to care for herself, including learning how to drive.

Matteo closed the door and jogged around to the passenger side.

"Where are we going?" Norma asked when they pulled away from the curb.

"To the hospital," Celeste replied as she came to a complete stop at the corner. She counted to three before making a right turn.

"We're going to visit Cousin Georgia?"

"No, we need to see Matteo's father. He got sick, so they took him to the hospital."

"I'm sorry about your father." A small hand settled on Matteo's shoulder. "I hope he feels better soon."

The lump that formed in Matteo's throat made it impossible to vocalize his gratitude. He reached up and patted the hand of the child who inspired so much in so many people.

Bailey credited Norma for inspiring her to get first her high school and then her college degrees. The girl was also one of the reasons Matteo had stayed clean.

Hours after Norma was born, Matteo had returned to the hospital to check on Bailey. Before he left, the nurse insisted on showing him the baby.

One look at her brown eyes, chubby cheeks, and

cupid-bow mouth and he understood how parents could have room in their hearts for more than one child. She was not his daughter, yet he cared for her as much as he did Julia. The fondness grew when she was ten months old and repeated Julia's "Da-da" when he walked into the kitchen during a family gathering. When she was older, Bailey instructed the girl to call him "Mr. Matteo." However, the pride he'd felt when she used the term of endearment never left him.

Being denied access to one daughter broke his heart. He could not give Bailey a reason to withhold visitation rights to Norma. That would destroy him.

They arrived at the hospital and Matteo jumped out of the car before Celeste had shifted into park. He dashed across the street, into the building, and down the hall to the waiting room.

His eldest brother, Stefan, was the first to glance up from comforting their mother. The tenderness in his eyes vanished. A dark cloud covered his features as he rose from his seat.

"How is he?" Matteo asked.

"You're not welcome here." Raymond Santiano's voice echoed from down the hall.

Matteo spun around to face the second son born to Angelo and Anna Santiano. Raymond's twin, Carmine, was steps behind him.

"He's my father," Matteo replied.

"You lost the right to call him that when you broke his heart." Carmine stopped in front of him and pointed towards the exit. "You need to leave."

"I'm not going anywhere," Matteo insisted.

In three strides, Stefan moved from the far corner of the room to the doorway. He shoved Matteo, who instinctively pushed back. Carmine and Raymond grabbed his arms, but before fists could fly, their mother's voice echoed in the hall.

"Stop it. Now!"

The struggle ceased. Everyone watched as the woman shuffled towards the group. A bout of polio had slowed the small woman's steps, yet Matteo saw stars when her palm connected with his face.

"Your father was generous to spare your life, but that did not absolve you of all your sins." Despite the pain in her gray eyes, her voice did not crack. "You're no longer a part of this family." Her tone was as firm as his father's had been when he made the same declaration two years earlier.

The words struck Matteo harder than the slap. It felt like someone plunged a knife into his chest and then, for kicks, turned it to shred his heart.

Matteo searched the faces of the people he'd grown up with. There was no sympathy for him, only disdain. Thanks to his stupidity, he could not be there for the man who had given him life.

With a growl, he slammed his fist into the wall before he marched past Celeste and Norma and out of the hospital.

****

Suspecting he would not answer, Bailey did not bother to knock. She simply pushed open the door and stepped into the room illuminated by the scant glow from the streetlight on the corner.

Matteo stared at the bottle of whiskey cradled in his hand. Though his possession of alcohol was not ideal, it was better than the drugs Celeste had suggested he would go in search of when she ran up to the maternity ward to inform Bailey of the incident in the hospital's waiting room.

He did not move as she closed the door and walked across the room. She pulled the second chair out from the table and sat in front of him.

"You're going to drink that?" she asked.

"I haven't decided," Matteo mumbled.

She grasped the neck of the bottle. "Let me help you make up your mind." He offered no resistance as she took the alcohol away from him. "This isn't the answer."

"Then what is? Time? Patience?" He slammed a hand on the table. "They won't let me see my father. He could be dying, yet they won't let me see him."

"Celeste provided updates during the day." Bailey set the bottle aside. "It was a mild heart attack. Your father will be fine."

She leaned forward in the chair and wrapped a hand around his. Matteo's head fell forward. A drop splattered over her fingers.

Bailey leaned in and wrapped both arms around his shoulders. His body shook as his tears soaked the collar of her dress.

She offered no words. Anything she said would sound like bullshit.

After her parents kicked her out, her cousin had tried to comfort her and offer hope they would come around. Yet nothing made her feel better. She did not want to wish for them to be in her life in the future. She had wanted them there at that moment.

As he had done for her days earlier, Bailey held him until he was all cried out. When there was nothing left inside, he pulled back and stared at her.

"Why'd you come here?" He made no attempt to

wipe away the tears staining his cheeks and showed no shame for having broken down in front of her.

"You were there for me whenever I needed someone," Bailey replied. "I can't walk away when you're most alone."

Matteo threw in a ragged breath. For years he had been the strong one, steady and unshakable, offering her strength. She just hoped she could repay him in his time of need.

Matteo cupped her face in her hand. He leaned in until his lips brushed against hers. The first touch was soft, almost cautious, as if he was afraid she would also reject him. When she did not pull away, he kissed her again, firmer, more demanding.

Since they had come together in the back of the diner, Bailey had been listing the reasons why being with Matteo was wrong. Mainly, after all they had done for her, she could not betray the Santianos by getting together with the enemy.

A part of her had been happy when he did not stop by the diner the next day or the day after. The coward in her hoped he had run off again, freeing her from having to tell him what they both knew...they could not see each other anymore.

Matteo's hand brushed against her breast. She knew she would never find the strength to walk away from him. He was everything she had ever wanted in a man— he was hardworking, kind, supportive and, most importantly, accepting of her daughter. To top it off, he not only knew how to excite her, he knew how to satisfy her craving.

In tune to her needs, he reached under her dress and the layers of petticoats and tugged on her underwear. She raised her hips, and he slid them off her. He then pulled out his wallet and retrieved a condom, which impressed her the most. He was not going to be caught in a situation in which he had to choose between continuing while praying a little one would not be created or stopping when they needed it the most.

Together they unzipped his pants. She released him from the confines of his clothes and rolled on the condom. He urged her forward, until she was straddling his lap. She guided him to her opening and then released a sigh as he slowly filled her.

Though they were fully clothed...minus her underwear...sitting in his combination living room/dining room/kitchen, it was more intimate than being with him in the diner. They held each other and said with their eyes, everything they were reluctant to vocalize. And, when they came, they witnessed every shudder the other experienced when reaching the final peak.

When the trembles ceased, there was no rush to break their hold and straighten their clothes. She laid her head on his shoulder and listened to his sighs of satisfaction as his heartbeat soothed her.

She would not read more into their coming together. It was not about getting to know one another or building a relationship. He had been offering comfort at the diner when the moment happened, just as she was comforting him in the apartment.

****

Matteo rolled over and his heart stopped. Afraid he had crushed Bailey, he dropped back onto his side of the bed.

A second passed before the cobwebs in his brain

cleared and he realized he was alone. He glanced around the room as he listened for the slightest sound that would indicate her presence. But even as he strained to hear a breath, he knew his actions were in vain.

She had slipped out while he slept. He was certain she had a good excuse for her absence, but it did not matter. He did not appreciate waking up in a bed by himself, not when the woman who meant so much to him had fallen asleep next to him.

Chapter Eighteen

Matteo slumped in the chair with his arms crossed over his chest and his bottom lip protruding, reminding Bailey of a boy who was denied the toy truck he coveted. She pocketed a tip left by a regular, then moved to the corner table outside her section.

"What's eating you?" she asked.

"I don't like waking up by myself," Matteo replied.

"What do you expect me to do about that?"

"Don't leave my bed in the middle of the night."

The gasp from the woman behind her reminded Bailey theirs was not an appropriate conversation for the diner. However, since Matteo did not seem concern about airing his business in public, and Bailey had nothing to be ashamed of, she replied, "I needed to get back to Norma. I promised to tuck her in before she went to sleep."

Though he did not challenge her excuse, he stared at her as if he knew there was more, which, of course, there was.

The Santianos had opened their home to protect Norma and her. How could she repay them by sleeping with the person who was as good as dead to them?

"I'm not having this conversation with you here." She tapped on the menu the other waitress had left him. "What do you want?"

"Somone to warm my bed at night and be there in

211

the morning," Matteo replied.

Bailey shoved her notepad into her apron pocket. "When you're ready to order, you know where to find me." She turned to get the coffeepot from behind the counter to refill the cup another diner shook at her.

She had taken two steps when the front door opened and Nicholas walked in.

"What are you doing here?" Bailey asked, reversing directions. "Is everyone all right?"

Matteo leaned forward, straining to hear the news.

"Georgia had twins…a boy and a girl," Nicholas replied. "Everyone's fine."

Before she could celebrate, Bailey asked, "What about your uncle?"

"He looked better this morning. The doctors expect to send him home in a few days."

Matteo released the breath he had been holding and dropped his head into his hands. Bailey patted his shoulder, trying to offer him what little comfort she could give in public.

Nicholas's gaze shifted to her hand. He frowned yet refrained from commenting. Instead, he asked, "Can I get a cup of coffee to go?"

"Have you eaten?" Bailey asked.

Nicholas shook his head.

"I'll make you a sandwich."

"Can you make it quick? I wanna get back to the hospital."

Ignoring the grumbling of the thirsty customer, Bailey stepped into the kitchen. "Georgia had twins," she announced, grabbing two slices of bread from the counter.

"Congratulations," Anita said. "Everyone's fine?"

"According to Nick, yes."

"I hope she takes advantage of her stay in the hospital. Once she gets home, it's gonna be nonstop."

Bailey could only imagine. When she was not feeding, changing, or comforting Norma, she had been preparing bottles, washing diapers, and keeping house. The only time she had to rest was when Norma took her naps.

For her cousin's sake, she prayed the children stayed on the same schedule so their mother would have some time to herself.

"So, what's going on with your man?" Anita asked. "He looks like a bulldog with his bottom lip poking out. He's scaring away my customers."

Bailey tilted her head to the side and raised an eyebrow. The diner was as busy as any other Saturday morning. The difference was the girls who usually giggled and vied for Matteo's attention had taken one look at his grimace, and scurried to the other end of the dining room to whisper amongst themselves until it was time to head to the movies.

"He's in a mood today."

"Well, tell him to take his mood somewhere else."

Bailey nodded as she wrapped up the ham-and-cheese sandwich for Nicholas. She returned to the dining room and passed him the food, then poured his coffee. When she turned back to him, he held out a dollar to her.

"Keep the change," Nicholas said when she took the money.

"Thanks."

He took the coffee, turned to Matteo, and jerked his head towards the door. The sullen man stood and walked out, saving Bailey from having to extend an invitation for him to vacate the premises.

****

"What the hell were you thinking last night?" Nicholas asked, climbing behind the wheel of his convertible.

"I was thinking my father was in the hospital and I should be there for him," Matteo replied, slipping into the passenger seat of the vehicle identical to the one he used to own. The month after they said, "I do," Eleanor had driven his car to the dealer to trade it for what she had considered a more sensible model. That had been the first night of many where he had walked away from home to keep from wrapping his hands around her throat.

When Bailey had told him Georgia insisted Nicholas keep his treasured car, Matteo prayed his cousin appreciated the woman who not only claimed she loved him, but who respected him and his possessions, too.

Nicholas passed the paper cup to Matteo. "You're lucky your brothers didn't give you a reason to check in." He unwrapped the sandwich and bit off a considerable chunk. "You know the family's code. Once you're out…"

Matteo did not need his cousin to spell out the consequences of screwing over the family or breaking one of their commandments. While unwritten, the rules were firmly established and drilled into each of them from childhood. The fact that he was still breathing was a miracle. He should be grateful for what he had and not covet any more. But he could not help but want to be a part of the family…to be welcomed and accepted by not only his parents and siblings, but the woman who always seemed to be out of his reach.

"I haven't always seen eye to eye with Pops, but I

can't imagine what it'd be like if I couldn't talk to him. Hopefully those snots your brothers sired will learn from your mistake."

The possibility the consequences he was suffering would be a warning to others did not make him feel better.

"Did you come to rub salt in my wounds?" Matteo asked.

Nicholas pointed to the glove compartment as he took another bite. Matteo opened the small door and pulled out a slip of paper. He read the two addresses scribbled on the sheet while his cousin chewed.

"That's the information you wanted," Nicholas said after he swallowed. "Sorry I couldn't get it to you sooner, but, you know, with Georgia and the babies..."

Matteo did not need an explanation. His cousin's wife had and always would come first.

Nicholas took the coffee back. "Do you need any help?"

Matteo shook his head. He did not want to share the satisfaction he would get from avenging Bailey's attack.

"A word of advice," his cousin said. "Bailey and Norma can't replace Eleanor and Julia."

"I'm not trying to replace Eleanor." Matteo would never try to replace something he was never fond of to begin with.

Eleanor had been a drunken one-night stand he married out of obligation. He never promised her more than his name and financial security.

What he was doing was setting himself up for heartbreak. No matter how much he wanted it, he could not be with Bailey while he was considered an outcast with his family.

Sure, they had come together twice. But, when she was tired of sneaking a moment here and there, she would find someone who could offer her a happily-ever-after, and he would be forced to watch from the sidelines.

"And I'd never try to replace Julia," he added before he climbed out of the car and strolled to the bus stop.

Replacing Julia would be like trying to replace a limb. While the prosthetic could help the user function, it was not the same as the real thing.

No, he had room in his heart for more than one child…even if the child did not come from his loins.

By the time he disembarked from the bus two stops before he normally got off with Bailey, he had committed the address to memory. He marched to the building, ignoring those who felt the need to gawk at the lighter man who dared to trespass in their neighborhood.

Matteo entered the building at the same time an older woman opened a door to the rear apartment on the first floor. She glanced at him over the head of a young boy, yanked the child back into the apartment and slammed the door.

As he ran up the steps two at a time, deadbolts clicked and chains slid into place on doors that were only locked when the residents were planning to be away from the building for an extended period. The sound assured him no one would interfere with his business, no matter what they heard. It also warned him no help would come if he was not successful.

Matteo stopped when he reached the first door on the third floor. The apartment's location gave the resident the advantage of seeing who was entering and exiting the building—a disadvantage for anyone hoping to surprise him. The other drawback was the front of the building offered too many witnesses who might provide information to the law if the man who used the apartment for work, rest, and play jumped out—with a little assistance, of course..

Figuring he would deal with the problems if they arose, Matteo pounded on the door. The gurgle of a flushing toilet and the clanging pipes offered him some hope the man he was looking for had not witnessed his arrival.

"Who's there?" The deep voice called out.

"I've a message from Lincoln," Matteo replied.

He counted to one as the cylinder in the deadbolt disengaged, two as the latch slid back, and three as he threw his weight against the door, snapping the flimsy chain that was supposed to keep intruders out.

Chapter Nineteen

The bruise on Matteo's left cheek would have stirred Bailey's sympathy had she not first seen the blood covering the knuckles on his right hand. While he was a little worse for wear, she had a feeling the recipient of the beating looked three times worse.

He passed her the Con Edison bill, the magazine Norma had been looking forward to since she finished reading the previous month's issue, and the small weekly magazine she had been subscribing to since its debut seven years earlier.

"You can move back home whenever you're ready, Shorty," Matteo announced.

"Thank you." His use of her nickname offered Bailey hope that he was in a better mood. "Now that you've had a chance to blow off some steam, you finished pouting?"

"No."

Bailey sighed. She already had one child to deal with and had little patience for an overgrown one.

"What do you want?" she asked, giving him one last chance to reasonable before she slammed the door in his face.

"One night." He stepped forward until barely an inch separated them. "Just you and me."

The warmth from his body stirred the memories of their last time together. There had not been much in the way of foreplay, yet he brought her to an orgasm that made her toes curl. When he finally carried her to bed, he'd held her close, silently conveying how much he wanted her.

She too wanted more than a quickie in a storage room or an hour in his arms. But if she got her wish, would she be satisfied when they went back to the way things were?

****

Liar, echoed in Matteo's brain.

No matter how much he tried to convince himself one night would suffice, he knew a single get-together would not be enough. Once he had a taste of what it would be like to make love to Bailey until they were sated, fall asleep with her in his arms, then wake up with her beside him, he would want more.

Celeste stepped into the doorway. "You should go. After everything that's happened, you deserve a night out." She patted Bailey's hand.

Matteo raised an eyebrow at his cousin, silently wondering what the woman was up to. Though she'd called him after Bailey had been attacked, he knew she did not trust him.

"I'll watch Norma," Celeste added.

"But what about—" Bailey started.

"If anyone asks, I'll tell them you went out with a friend."

Bailey hesitated for a second before her head slowly moved up and down. "I need to let Norma know I'm going out." She squeezed Celeste's hand. "Thank you."

"Put on shoes you can walk in," Matteo said.

"Why?" Bailey asked.

"It's a surprise," he replied.

If he was going to have one night with her, he was going to make damn well sure it was special. Though they would eventually end up in bed together, he did not want to spend all their time there.

Matteo cupped her neck with his hand. His fingers teased the short, fine hairs along her nape. "I want tonight to be memorable," he insisted, before brushing his lips over hers.

She lifted onto the tips of her toes and pressed closer to him. There was a familiar stirring in his pants. They would need to break it off or else their time together would be cut short when they were arrested for lewd behavior.

Matteo pulled back. Bailey dropped onto her heels and stared up at him, panting. The longing in her eyes could not be missed, but it had to be ignored.

"Get changed," he said.

Bailey stepped back into the house. As the tap of her shoes on the steps faded, Celeste cleared her throat. Her arms were folded across her chest.

"What?" Matteo asked.

"She trusts you," Celeste replied. "If you betray that trust, Nicholas is going to be the last person you'll need to worry about." The cold, steady delivery of the threat made him flinch.

Celeste was a few inches shorter than he was and several pounds lighter. There was a time when he could toss her over his shoulder and laugh as her tiny fists beat against his back. Her frown warned him those days had passed. He did not know what she thought she could do to him, and he was not willing to find out.

Having let him know her feelings, his cousin backed up into the house and closed the door. While he waited,

Matteo took advantage of an open fire hydrant two doors down to rinse the blood from his hands and the sweat from his brow. He dried his hands on his jeans before he sat on the stoop and lit a cigarette.

When Matteo used to wine and dine women, it was more like a mating ritual…he treated, and the females showed their gratitude. With Bailey, he hoped it would be different. He was not taking her out to get between her legs and she was not going out with him to get a free meal—or as in the case of his ex-wife, to land a husband. He enjoyed being with her, hearing her laughter, and watching her eyes light up when she was happy.

"Where are we going?" Bailey asked, stepping from the house.

He took in her canvas shoes and nodded his approval. "Coney Island," he replied, pushing up from his perch.

"But I thought we were taking Norma there."

"We can take her another time." He enclosed her hand in his. "I want to experience this with you."

The hour-long train ride offered Matteo an opportunity to discover the other attractions Bailey had not been able to enjoy in the eight years she'd lived in New York. She had not ventured farther than the neighborhoods where she lived, worked or attended classes. And, though he had asked for one night, he began planning future excursions for them around the city.

They got off the train at the last stop. Outside the Coney Island-Stillwell Avenue station, Bailey's gaze darted about, trying to take in all the sights at once.

"Where do you wanna start, Shorty?" he asked, draping an arm around her shoulders.

"There's so much," she replied as they crossed the street. "What do you recommend?"

He pointed to the Cyclone as a car dropped from the highest peak. "I could never get enough of the roller coaster when I was a kid."

Bailey shuddered. "Are you kidding?" She shook her head. "Is that even safe?"

"Of course, it is," Matteo chuckled. "Not even curious?"

She swallowed hard as the car sped over the wooden track. "Not the slightest."

Matteo mentally scratched the more daring rides off the list of attractions they would try. He had seen many young men tease and coax squeamish dates onto rides they were too nervous to try. Spending the evening trying to calm a hysterical woman—or worse, have her abandon him because he pressured her to do something—did not make for a memorable trip.

Deciding to start their evening with dinner, he led her to the hot dog stand. As they ate, Matteo reminisced about the contests he and his brothers would have to see who could eat the most hot dogs. When they could no longer tolerate the taste of the meat, they would head off to stuff their faces with popcorn, cotton candy, and caramel apples, then challenge each other to see who could stomach the most rides.

His brothers usually bowed out after two rides; their complexions a shade of green that would have other visitors cutting a wide berth around them to avoid being splattered by the inevitable regurgitation that spewed from the boys' mouths.

Nicholas, who usually joined them, lasted longer than any of them. His cousin would jump from one ride to the next until Matteo's father announced it was time to go.

They finished their hot dogs, and Matteo led Bailey to the carousel, which he recalled she enjoyed during their visit to the zoo a few weeks earlier. They spent the remainder of the afternoon dividing their time between strolls along the boardwalk and rides that did not move too fast or go too high. And since a trip to Coney Island would not be complete without indulging in treats, he purchased candy apples and cotton candy for them to share.

"Before we leave, you need to see the view from the Wonder Wheel," Matteo said.

Bailey glanced in the direction he pointed. "Why?" Her eyes widened as she stared at the Ferris wheel. "The view looks fine from the ground."

"It's even more spectacular from above."

****

Bailey's curiosity was piqued. Could the view be as breathtaking as Matteo made it out to be?

The riders squealed as their cars swayed back and forth. The noise did not help convince her…she did not normally shriek when she was having a good time.

Unlike the teenage boy ahead of them in line, who teased his companion and called her "chicken" until she gave in, Matteo silently waited for Bailey's answer. He was leaving the decision up to her, and she knew he would abide by whatever choice she made.

After praying Georgia would take in Norma, should anything go wrong with the ride, Bailey conceded with a nod. Matteo led her to the ticket booth and purchased two passes. They then stepped over to the next line, where he informed the ride operator they wanted a stationary car.

But once they were settled on the metal seat, she decided their definition of stationary did not agree with hers.

The car gently rocked back and forth as it slowly moved away from the ground. Her heart slammed in her chest. Her breathing became shallower. And every limb trembled.

It had been a mistake to get on the ride. Why had she not declined when Matteo insisted? It was not like he would have bullied her into doing what she did not want to do. He had proved what type of man he was when he dropped the subject of her trying the Cyclone without giving the ride a backwards glance.

Bailey flinched as a hand covered hers.

"It's okay." Matteo laid his free hand on her cheek and turned her head towards him. "It's gonna be all right."

He had made the promise to her so many times over the years, and each time he kept his word. She gently ran a finger over his battered knuckles, a result of his latest attempt to be there for her.

"You trust me?" he asked.

Bailey did not have to think about her answer. Matteo had never lied to her or given her cause not to trust him.

She nodded, confirming her belief in him.

Matteo dipped his head towards her. Their lips touched and all she could concentrate on was the slow stroke of his tongue against hers. Her heartbeat continued to race, not from fear but from the excitement building in her.

His arm snaked around her shoulders. She leaned against him. As always, she felt protected in his arms. No harm would come to her as long as he was by her side.

The ride stopped and Matteo broke the kiss. "Are you ready?" he asked, keeping his face close to hers.

Bailey took a deep breath and whispered, "Yes."

Matteo kept his arm around her as he sat back.

She gasped. He had been right. The view was incredible.

From the top of the Wonder Wheel, they could see everything—the children twirling around on the rides in the amusement parks, the families strolling on the boardwalk, and the couples lounging on beach.

"What do you think?" he asked.

"It's beautiful."

"Is this the right time to say, 'I told you so?'"

"No," Bailey replied, not wanting to give him the satisfaction.

Chuckling, he pressed his lips to hers, and her heart swelled with her desire for the man. Why did someone so right have to be off limits?

She lost herself in the kiss until a throat cleared, reminding her they were not in private. They pulled apart and encountered the disapproving glare of the ride operator. Yet, as the man had never done anything to advance the quality of her life, Bailey did not give a hoot about his opinion of them or their actions.

Matteo climbed out of the car and held out his hand. She intertwined her fingers with his, then allowed him to escort her through the amusement park to the street, where he hailed a cab.

Though the drive was quicker than taking the train, the half-hour trip took too long for her tastes. The kiss on the Wonder Wheel had made her eager to be with him.

They arrived at his apartment and Bailey's excitement turned to jitters. Their relationship was about to take a turning point and, no matter how much they tried to convince themselves otherwise, they would not be content with one night.

"You said you were taking me somewhere special," she teased.

"This is special," he replied. "I've never brought a woman here."

Bailey rolled her eyes. "You expect me to believe you haven't been with another woman?"

"Of course, I've been with other women. I just never brought them here."

A spark of jealousy ignited within her at the thought of him with anyone else. They were not committed to each other, and the chances of them having a long-term relationship were slim to none, but she did not like sharing.

****

A deep frown distorted Bailey's plump lips and a cloud settled over her features. Matteo understood the anger she felt when he confirmed there had been other women. It was the same he experienced whenever she went out with another man. However, he would not have her start an argument with him when he had been forced to suffer through her relationships in silence.

"You're not exactly a blushing virgin," Matteo said.

Though the statement was true, he instantly regretted having said it.

Bailey's frown shifted to a scowl. She turned to the door and her hand wrapped around the knob.

Matteo reached over her shoulder and placed his palm against the wood. "I'm sorry," he said, praying she didn't insist on leaving. "We only have this one night to be together. Let's not waste it fighting." He added, "*Per favore, amore mio.*" For though they did not have a future together, she would always be his love.

Bailey's head fell forward. Her shoulders drooped, but she did not pull on the door.

Hoping to convince her to stay and finish what they came to his apartment to do, he nuzzled the spot behind her right ear that had her trembling in his arms the previous night. She sighed, a deep sigh. Her head rose and her back arched.

His hand dropped from the door to her waist. He gently turned her until he could reach her lips. When her hand released the doorknob and gripped him, he knew he had her.

Chapter Twenty

Matteo was too sure of himself and needed to be taken down a peg. Thankfully, Bailey was up for the challenge.

"Prove it," she said to his assertion he knew all her secrets.

Matteo leaned on one elbow and fingered a strand that had worked loose from her French roll. "Orange is your favorite color, chocolate ice cream is your favorite food, and autumn is your favorite season."

He was correct on all aspects, but she was not ready to concede. "Lucky guess."

The hair slipped from his fingers, and he slid his hand from her neck to her breasts. "Then how 'bout this—you despise the color green, you would not touch a beet if your life depended on it, and you'd rather scrub lime from a bathtub than work with numbers."

Bailey rolled onto her side, her brow furrowed. "How'd you know?"

He could have overheard her complaining to Georgia that her mother used to knit her a green sweater every Christmas though she'd expressed her distaste for the color to the woman quite clearly. And, he could have seen her pass on the vile purple vegetables when she joined his family for dinner. But she did not recall ever expressing in words or actions her dislike for numbers.

"Whenever you did your homework, your face

scrunched up like someone slammed your hand in a car door." Matteo brushed a finger across her forehead. "You're also dragging your feet about accepting the position at Pop's store."

His palm rested on her left breast. There was nothing sensual about the touch. It simply felt natural lying there.

"Why did you study accounting if you couldn't stand math?" he asked.

"I wanted to be more like Georgia," Bailey said.

"And what was wrong with being Bailey?"

"She isn't as sophisticated and smart at Georgia." Bailey sighed. "Basically, Georgia was every parent's dreams."

The disappointment she'd felt whenever her parents gushed about Georgia slammed down on her shoulders. No matter how hard she tried, nothing she did was praised. They would not even acknowledge the areas—like cooking and spelling—in which she excelled but her cousin fell short. "Figured if I earned the same degree as Georgia, then…well, maybe—"

"You can't live your life trying to please others." He dropped onto his back and pulled her over until she was lying half on him and half on the mattress. "They'll never be happy, and you'll be miserable."

His somber tone told her he spoke from experience. "Eleanor?"

"She was just one of many."

"Who else?"

He weaved his fingers through her hair and kneaded her scalp. His silence continued until she believed she had found a topic he was not comfortable sharing with her.

She was about to change the subject, when he

released a mournful sigh. "A small part of me was happy when Eleanor announced she was pregnant. Instead of going to grad school, I'd have to marry her and take care of the books at the shop."

Bailey tilted her head back until she could look him in the eye. No emotions could be detected on his face, yet the statement alone said he was serious.

"My family has a habit of planning the lives of their children and, like stooges, we go along with that," Matteo continued. "The only ones with the balls to do their own things were Nick and Celeste."

Unfortunately, things did not work out for Celeste. Less than six months after she'd become a bride, she lost a child, a husband, and her faith in humanity.

Nicholas had found some success as a bookie. When he decided to marry Georgia, he gave up his business to run the restaurant his father originally intended for him to take over.

"A month after I started the second grade, my teacher scheduled a meeting with my parents to announce I was ahead of the class. I had started the day in one grade, skipped two by noon, and had my future planned for me by the time I got home." Matteo chuckled. "Before then, I wasn't much of a fighter, but tossed in with twenty-two students who were bigger than me, I quickly learned."

Bailey understood his need to find a silver lining in a stressful situation, yet she could not smile at the thought of a boy being forced to learn how to defend himself from bullies, even if his acquired skill had helped her more than once.

"My father decided I was going to get a master's degree and be an engineer." Matteo continued. "But by the time I completed my freshman year of college I was tired of studying."

Having witnessed how stubborn the Santianos could be, Bailey did not bother to ask why he did not tell anyone. Once they set their minds on something, only a decree from their Maker could change it.

"I wish I'd had the balls then to stand up to Pops and tell him I didn't want to live his dreams," Matteo added.

There was no guarantee following his own dreams would have made him happy, but it sure as hell would have saved everyone some heartache.

"Miss North is retiring and Clara thought I'd like working at the library," Bailey confessed the decision she had been struggling to make.

Matteo cocked an eyebrow. "Do you want to be a librarian?"

Her head bobbed up then down. She enjoyed the children, got along with the employees, and loved the idea of working around books.

"Then what's stopping you?"

"It would require me to go back to school."

"And?"

"Norma had to put up with so much in order for me to get my bachelor's. Would it be fair to ask her to go through that for another two years?" Bailey asked.

"Would it be fair to her if you came home miserable every night from a job you can't tolerate?" Matteo stroked her cheek. "You owe it to yourself to do something that makes you happy. Both of you will reap the rewards from it."

Bailey sighed. Okay, he wasn't just talk. He knew her secrets and was a sage advisor. Of course, he wasn't the only one with knowledge.

Bracing her arms on his chest, she locked eyes with Matteo. "So, when do you plan on telling me you've been my landlord for the past six years?"

****

Matteo's hand froze at the edge of her jaw. "Mr. Roberts told you?"

"He confirmed my suspicions when I asked," Bailey replied.

"How long have you known?"

"I first suspected something when you told me you found a place I'd like at a price I could afford. Nine months after I moved in, I found the rent envelope I had given Mr. Roberts in your glove compartment. When I asked him who owned the building, he confirmed you did."

"Why didn't you tell me you knew?"

"At the time, I was afraid of what you'd do. The week before I found the envelope, we were attending Nonna's birthday party, and Eleanor told everyone you returned a set of earrings you bought her."

Matteo closed his eyes and sighed at his ex-wife's complaint. The woman had conveniently left out the part about her criticizing the jewelry because they were one-caret diamonds, not two.

"I couldn't take a chance you'd rescind the offer," Bailey continued. "On my salary, I couldn't afford to go to school *and* pay what landlords are asking for decent apartments."

Matteo's spirits sank. Just as he never wanted her to think his gifts came with conditions or expectations of something in return, he did not want her to fear retaliation from him.

His arms encircled her shoulders and held her tight.

He had been such a jerk; he shouldn't have questioned what it would take to win her over. He should've been asking why she stuck by him in the first place.

Chapter Twenty-One

Bailey laughed when Matteo nudged her away from the stove with his hip and mumbled, "My stove," like a child protective of a treasured toy.

"You're kind of selfish for someone with three brothers," Bailey said, stepping away from the appliance whose style had been discontinued the year she was born. Nothing in the apartment had been made in that decade, yet the care put into restoring each piece demonstrated a remarkable amount of patience by the owner.

"Spent too many years sharing." He flipped a pancake on the cast-iron griddle. "Won't do it unless I've no other choice."

She moved to his left, reached around him, and swiped a strip of bacon off the plate sitting on the back of the stove. As she backed away, Matteo grabbed the front of the t-shirt she had slipped on, pulled her against him and kissed her deeply.

He tasted of mouthwash and cigarette smoke and smelled like the all-purpose soap she used to clean her dishes.

"I don't like your outfit," he said when he pulled away to rescue the overcooked pancake.

"You don't want me wearing your clothes?" Bailey had not thought he would have a problem with her slipping on the shirt he'd dropped on the floor before they climbed into bed the previous night.

"I prefer you in nothing."

"I don't make it a habit of going into the kitchen without clothes." Her gaze shifted to the green boxers covering Matteo's assets. A daring outfit when there was the potential for grease splatter. "Now, what can I do to help?"

He raised both eyebrows.

"And I'm not taking my clothes off…"

Bailey was grateful for her decorum when the door swung open and a teenage boy burst into the room.

"Get this, Matte…" He froze in the threshold and gawked at the shirt that stopped mid-thigh on Bailey.

Matteo rolled his eyes before pouring more batter onto the pan. Since he was not going to make a big deal about their state of undress, Bailey decided to follow his example and play it cool. She swiped another strip of bacon, then positioned herself behind a chair.

"You're gonna keep standing there and let the flies in?" Matteo's voice was steady as if he were in his work clothes instead of standing half-naked in his kitchen with a woman in a similar state of undress.

The boy stepped into the apartment, closed the door, and shoved his hands into the front pockets of jeans that had worked as hard as the wearer.

"Introduce yourself," Matteo ordered.

"Uh…uh…" The noise reminded her of the seals they'd seen at the zoo weeks earlier. The boy's cheeks reddened. He snapped his mouth shut and took a deep breath before he croaked. "I'm Liam…Liam Murphy."

Bailey held out her hand and replied, "I'm Bailey. It's nice meeting you."

Liam gaped at her palm until Matteo nudged the boy on the shoulder. His arm shot up and he grasped Bailey's hand in a firm grip. "Nice meeting you," he replied, pumping her arm up and down.

"Whaddya want?" Matteo asked.

"I dropped by to shoot the breeze. You know, like we do every Sunday."

Both of Matteo's eyebrows shot up. Apparently, the frequency of their conversations was news to him.

Liam jerked his head towards the door with all the subtlety of a pimp in an orange suit and green tie.

Deciding to take pity on the boy before he suffered from whiplash, Bailey announced, "I'll wait for you in the other room." She tugged her arm back. "My hand."

The boy released her. "Oh, sorry." His blush grew darker.

Matteo's smirk faded and his eyes narrowed. Though she was also disappointed by the interruption, she gently shook her head, silently warning him to be nice to the kid.

****

Matteo sighed. The kid had a lot to learn.

He silently debated where to begin—not ogling another man's woman or recognizing the clues that suggested his presence wasn't welcome at the moment.

"Whaddya want?" He repeated his question.

The lectures could wait until another day—when a half-naked Bailey was not waiting for him in the next room.

"I asked her out last night," Liam replied when the bedroom door closed.

"Who?"

"That girl…um…you know. The one I liked."

"I'm assuming she said yes?"

Grinning from ear to ear, the boy furiously nodded

his head.

Matteo rolled his eyes. He would not have been as forgiving had he been the one accosted by some punks while the kid did nothing but watch.

"She wasn't sure, when I first asked," Liam said.

"What changed her mind?" Matteo asked.

Liam pointed to the eye that still sported a faint bruise. "She was impressed I stood up for her last week."

"Where'd you go?"

"I took her to a movie and then a burger."

"And then?"

The boy's grin grew wider and goofier. "I kissed her good night." His smile vanished and he quickly he added, "But I asked if it was all right with her first."

Maybe there was hope for the kid. With a bit more guidance there was a possibility he would not make the same mistakes as Matteo.

"Anyway, I just wanted to tell you that." He stepped back. "I won't keep you from your company."

"Thank you."

"You're coming to dinner?"

Matteo would have liked Mrs. Murphy to meet Bailey, but he had to get her back to Norma. "Another time."

With a wave, Liam ducked out of the apartment. The door clicked shut before the kid was halfway down the hall, yet the sound of his heavy tread on the stairs broke through the barrier.

Matteo finished preparing breakfast. As he reached up into the cabinet to grab two plates, he came up with a better idea. He closed the doors, grabbed two forks from the drawer next to the sink, and carried the dish that had been warming on the back of the stove to the bedroom.

Bailey sat cross-legged in the center of the bed, reading an issue of *Popular Mechanics* she'd taken from the top of the stack of magazines on his nightstand's lower shelf.

She pointed to the mountain of pancakes and bacon. "You're feeding an army?"

"Figured you worked up an appetite."

Tilting her head to the side and giving a shrug, she closed the magazine and leaned across the bed to place it back with the other issues. The t-shirt she wore rose an inch, offering him a glimpse of the firm, round cheek he had kneaded and kissed as he explored every inch of her last night.

Matteo's groan did not go unnoticed. Bailey peered over her shoulder and raised an eyebrow.

"You always had a problem following directions?" he asked, setting the tray on the dresser pushed against the wall to the right of the bedroom door.

"What?"

"You're still wearing clothes."

Bailey knelt on the bed. Her smirk said she had not tired of him yet. And, in case he did not get the message, the shirt flying over her head and dropping to the floor by his feet told him what was to come.

****

"Liam's lucky to have you as a role model," Bailey praised after Matteo recounted the boy's ongoing encounter with the young lady.

Matteo shrugged a shoulder as he reached for a slice of bacon that had grown cold while they enjoyed each other's company. "He could've done worse."

"You've got to stop putting yourself down." Her foot caressed his bare calf. "You made a mistake. You

238

can't keep beating yourself up for it."

It was hard not to kick himself when he looked at the mess he had made, not only of his own life but the lives of those close to him. He'd disappointed his parents, hurt Eleanor and Julia, and ruined any possibility of a relationship with Bailey.

"Look at how far you have come. You've cleaned yourself up and you finally found your purpose." Bailey waved a hand around the room. "This building used to be a place where people simply laid their heads at night. However, since you took over the management of the property, it has become a home for every tenant who lives here."

It was the least he could do after neglecting the property he had purchased from the same man who sold him Bailey's place. Instead of caring for his investment, he'd placed the control in the hands of manager, who overcharged the tenants, ignored repairs, and allowed unsavory characters to run illicit activities from several of the apartments. When he finally got clean and checked on the building, he had been so ashamed of the conditions the honest tenants had been forced to live under, he vowed to turn the place around with his own hands.

"You're not just a super. You're a big brother to Liam and another grandson to his grandmother. And I'm sure if you spoke to the other tenants, you'd find you're much more to them, too."

A lump formed in the back of Matteo's throat. Her words offered him hope that a day would come when he could make things right with the people he'd hurt, gain their forgiveness and, most importantly, forgive himself.

Chapter Twenty-Two

Bailey's heart sank when she stepped into the apartment. She was grateful Matteo had convinced her to head home and straighten up before Celeste dropped off Norma. Her daughter did not need to see the destruction that waited for them.

She kicked the torn chair cushion lying on the floor and shook her head.

"There's no way I'm gonna get this cleaned up before Norma gets home."

"*We* can do it if *we* work together," Matteo offered.

Indeed, together they had accomplished so much over the years. She may have been the one who made up her mind to go back to school, who went to the classes and studied until she was cross-eyed. Yet he tutored her on the subjects she had problems with and encouraged her throughout the process.

With a nod of her head, she set an end table upright and dropped her purse on top. Matteo picked up the cushion and propped it against the wall.

For the next three hours, they bagged broken knickknacks, rehung clothes, and pushed damaged furniture into the hall. By the time they were finished, Bailey's spirits had sunk farther.

Not a dish had survived being pulled from the cabinets and tossed onto the floor. Several of Norma's toys had been broken when her toybox was overturned.

And all the upholstery had been slashed beyond repair.

Thankfully, she had been staying with the Santianos. From the destruction, there was no doubt the intruder would not have hesitated to harm Norma or her to locate whatever he was searching for.

They did not find a clue as to who was responsible for the break-in and there was no way of knowing if he'd found what he was looking for or if he would return when he was certain the residents had settled back in.

Bailey shivered. Was it safe for Norma and her to move back in? What if it had not been her attacker who broke in? If it had been her brother, he was more dangerous than she'd initially wanted to believe. And, if that was the case, thanks to her insisting Matteo leave the man alone, he was out there, free to come back whenever he wanted.

"It's okay," Matteo whispered, encircling her with one arm.

She had not realized how much she depended on him to feel safe until he ran out to use the payphone on the corner. She needed to learn how to be comfortable in her own home again, fast. Norma needed a mother who was strong and sure of herself, not someone who jumped at every creak drip and groan in the house.

"I called in a few favors," Matteo replied when he returned. "The place will be as good as new in no time."

As usual, Matteo was a man of his word. Within an hour and a half, a moving van was parked outside the building and the damaged furniture had been carried out by men she had seen at a couple of the Santiano celebrations over the years. The new pieces that were left gave the space a different feeling.

"Wow," Norma exclaimed as she bounced into the

apartment and stared at the blue sectional sofa. "Can I sit on it?"

Matteo walked back into the house from the back yard where he had retreated while the movers were replacing the furniture. "You can sit on it, jump on it, whatever you want. It's yours."

"You will *not* jump on any furniture in the house," Bailey said when the girl sprinted from the room. She glared at the instigator of much of the mischief her daughter got into at home.

"Now that explains everything," Celeste said, passing Bailey her suitcase.

"Explains what?" Bailey asked.

"When he was nine, he fell off Nicky's bed. The bump must've knocked something loose in his head."

"If it did, I can assure you your father knocked it back in place," Matteo replied.

****

He had accepted Nicholas's challenge to a jumping contest, which ended after his foot got tangled in the blankets and he fell. Uncle Marco made sure there were no other bruises than the knot and carpet burn on his forehead, then smacked him upside the back of his head for attempting a foolish feat.

His father grounded him for two weeks and gave him extra chores at the store as punishment for disrespecting furniture.

Despite her tomboyish tendencies and his poor advice, Norma proved she could have just as much fun without destroying furniture. She raced back into the room and dropped her stuffed animals next to the rag doll she'd set on the sofa earlier, then assigned seats to the toys like a teacher arranging her students before she began showing the clues she had found.

Bailey nodded towards the rear of the apartment. Matteo waved his cousin forward, then took up the rear, leaving the girl to enjoy her living room for the first time in months.

"Are y'all staying for dinner?" Bailey asked, pulling out her cast-iron skillet.

Matteo shook his head. "You don't have to—"

"Yes, I do," she interrupted him. "Things have to get back to normal."

"It's gonna take more than a meal to get there." Celeste's voice cracked as she made her declaration.

Matteo repressed the urge to shush her. Bailey needed to hear the truth, and if anyone should know how much a trauma would affect her, it would be his cousin.

"For a while, you're gonna jump at the slightest noise. You'll be constantly looking over your shoulder and swear the shadows are moving. And there are times you'll wanna curl up into a ball and cry." Celeste took a ragged breath. "This is going to be your new normal. and I found it was easier to accept it than pretend everything's all right."

"Will it ever get easier?" Bailey asked.

"It may; it may not. I can't say for sure." Celeste shrugged. "I'd like to think it made me stronger."

Matteo could not say whether Celeste was stronger. She was no longer the happy-go-lucky girl he knew as a child. And, she had lost her ability to trust and forgive, the qualities he sometimes found frustrating in Bailey yet could never imagine her no longer possessing.

Chapter Twenty-Three

"Relax." Matteo draped his arm around Bailey, a move that went a long way towards ensuring she would not be able to obey his command.

Aside from those on the bus who appeared ready to express their displeasure at them being together, the intimate gesture stirred up memories of the time they'd spent together the previous weekend. He had asked for one night, and like a fool she'd tried to pretend it would be enough.

That one night was only a taste and, unlike a child who got too many bowls of the ice cream she craved, she would never get sick of him.

"What's wrong?" Matteo's finger traced the edge of her lobe.

Bailey shivered. The man was a quick study. He had taken his time to learn how to excite her and was willing to use the knowledge to distract her.

She took his hand and intertwined their fingers. She could not be distracted…not before she spoke her mind. "I wish you wouldn't take this chance."

Sighing, Matteo pulled his hand free and slipped his arm from around her shoulders. "I need to see my father."

"But I told you—"

"I need to see him with my own two eyes. You don't know what it's like not being able to see your parents."

"Excuse me?" Bailey leaned away from him and raised her eyebrows.

For eight years, her parents had refused to acknowledge her existence. Letters were returned unopened and pleas for phone calls were ignored.

"Sorry. Of course, you know what it's like." He picked her hand off her lap. "Then you should understand why I need to see him. You'd try to see your father under the same circumstances."

Bailey admitted she would try. The difference was she did not risk being placed in ICU for her efforts.

"How'd you find out your father was released from the hospital?"

"I stopped at the hospital on Saturday before I picked you up and paid a nurse to keep me updated on his condition. Besides, I knew he wouldn't miss the twins' coming-home party."

It was a popular sentiment.

According to Celeste, who had stopped by that morning to pick up Norma so the girl would not miss the babies' arrival, many friends and relatives had planned to drop by during the day to wish Georgia well.

"If it makes you feel better, I'll wait for you across the street."

It did not make her feel better. His family would object to his presence even if he was down the block. And there was no telling how he would react if Eleanor's friend was there.

Knowing nothing she said would dissuade him from trying to catch a glimpse of his father—and possibly end up with a busted lip for his efforts—she changed the subject. "What movie did you want to see?"

"I don't wanna go to the movies," he said. "How

'bout we take Norma to Coney Island?"

Bailey sighed. Matteo was offering her what she had wanted in the other men she had dated—except the freedom for them to be together.

They disembarked from the bus at the next stop. With no concern about the possibility of a family member driving by and catching them, Matteo held her hand as they strolled down the street. Bailey wished he would not take such chances. At the same time, she enjoyed the feeling of being part of a couple.

They turned the corner, and Matteo gave her hand a slight squeeze before he released her. He slowed his step, until he was two houses behind her. As she skipped across the street, he stopped next to a tree he could easily duck behind should someone look in his direction.

Outside Georgia's house, Julia played *Miss Mary Mack* with a cousin. The hand game took Bailey back to her youth when she would play with Georgia, whose hands flew as she sped through the rhyme. At that time, the only thing she had to worry about was Lincoln literally feeding her homework to their dog.

"Hi, Miss Collins," Julia greeted when they missed a clap.

"I used to play the same game when I was your age," she said.

"Cousin Georgia taught us."

"Norma's inside?" Bailey asked, glancing up at the house. Having inherited her cousin's coordination, Norma would never pass up an opportunity to play hand games.

"No, your brother picked her up," Eleanor announced as she emerged from the garden level. "He told her he was taking her to search for clues, though I didn't understand what that meant."

Bailey glimpsed around her nemesis through the window into the house. Surely the woman was joking. Norma was waiting for the right moment to jump out and yell *boo*.

One second, then two, then finally three passed. There was no exclamation, no laughter, and no girl.

When the realization sank in, Bailey screamed as her worst nightmare became reality.

****

Matteo ignored the driver who slammed on the brakes to avoid mowing him down. The screeching tires and the man's profanity were drowned out by the cry echoing in his head.

"What the hell are you doing here?" Louie pushed away from the car he'd been leaning against and jumped in Matteo's path.

Without breaking his stride, Matteo swung at the man foolish enough to get between him and Bailey. He stepped over the body that crumpled at his feet, his concerns for Bailey overriding the satisfaction he should have felt at belting his foe.

"What's going on?" He glanced at his daughter, who had ducked behind her mother. "Where's Norma?"

"Lincoln took her." Bailey wrung her hands. Unspent tears hovered at the brink of her eyes.

Celeste ran down the steps from the parlor level of Nicholas and Georgia's brownstone.

"I don't understand," Eleanor said. "What's wrong?"

"My brother's a junkie."

"I didn't know. Norma was happy to see him."

"She hadn't told her," Celeste announced, placing

her hands on Bailey's shoulder.

Matteo wanted to be the one to hold her and tell her everything would be okay. But wasting words and time would not get the girl back.

"Where's Nick?" he asked.

"He ran to the store," Celeste replied.

"Give me your keys."

His cousin pulled a set of keys from the front pocket of her dress and tossed them to him. Matteo dove into the Studebaker parked in front of his uncle's building, pausing only long enough to adjust the seat before screeching away from the curb.

Guilt weighed heavily on his shoulders. He should not have bowed down to Bailey's insistence he give her brother another chance. Yes, he had been given chances, but it had not come without harsh consequences…the harshest of which he was still suffering.

Matteo was grateful he had listened to his instinct and asked Nicholas to track down Lincoln's whereabouts after he located the man's supplier. It was better to have an address and not need it than to need the location and not have it.

Though he should not have expected more from a junkie who would kidnap his niece, Matteo was appalled by the decrepit dwelling nestled between two abandoned buildings near the waterfront. The rats engaged in a battle over the contents of an abandoned greasy bag scattered when he pulled up.

Matteo jumped from the car, ran into the building, and followed the dusty footprints up the wooden steps As he ascended each level, Norma's sobs grew louder.

He reached the fourth floor and the girl's wailed, "I wanna go home," tore at his heart. His blood boiled when her request was met with a growled, "Shut 'er up."

But he was taken back by the high-pitched, "I ain't know nuthin' 'bout no damn chill'in."

Whether Lincoln's accomplice knew anything about children or not, Matteo expected a woman to have more compassion for the child.

He moved to the open door at the end of the hall. He wasn't sure whether the occupants had been too high to notice the barrier hadn't been pushed completely closed or trusted no one would bother them in the isolated building. Either way, he was grateful he did not have to break down the door and could save his energy to pummel Bailey's brother.

He peered through the crack and spied Norma at the opposite end of the room. Her corkscrew curls had unraveled, a black streak stained the front of her yellow dress, and her right foot was minus a white patent leather shoe. Tears and dirt covered her face.

Satisfied the girl was nowhere near the impending battle, Matteo shoved the door open.

"What the hell?" the woman yelled.

Matteo ignored the owner of the high-pitched voice as he lunged towards Lincoln. The other man grabbed the piece lying next to his arm, aimed, and pulled the trigger.

There was a click instead of the expected bang. Lincoln's mouth dropped open. He glanced at the bullets scattered across the scratched and stained countertop.

Matteo's legs, shaky from the near call with the gun, barely supported him as he grabbed Lincoln's wrist and slammed his hand on the counter. The piece dropped to the floor and, with one kick, he sent in under the brown refrigerator.

Focused on the gun, Matteo had failed to watch the other man's free hand. Thankfully, he heard the whistle from the two-by-four swinging towards his head.

Matteo blocked the blow with his left arm. A pain sliced through his forearm. Bright stars obscure his vision.

He wanted to retreat to a corner and nurse his wound, yet he pushed the pain to the recesses of his mind as he blindly swung forward. He was rewarded by the feel of the other man's nose shifting beneath his fists. The sound of wood hitting linoleum indicated he had a second to regroup as Lincoln dealt with his wounds.

The stars faded as a familiar blonde bouffant rushed past Matteo. In her haste to flee, Bailey's neighbor tripped over her feet and fell into the door. Holding tight to the knob, she righted herself, then dashed into the hall. Blood dripped from between Lincoln's fingers as he stumbled behind her.

Matteo snatched the two-by-four from the floor and followed the couple. He caught up with the kidnappers in the hall and smacked the board against the back of Lincoln's skull.

Bailey's brother lurched forward. He grabbed the woman's arm. With a teeth-grinding squeal, she pulled away. She lost her balance and tumbled down the stairs.

Matteo tossed the board to the side. While it worked to daze his adversary, it was not as satisfying as the feel of his fist against the man's flesh.

He grabbed Lincoln by the collar and yanked him back, slammed him against the wall, and delivered a punch to his gut, followed by an uppercut.

Lincoln slid to the floor, where he curled into a ball, tucking his head into his chest. The submissive position did not faze Matteo. Bracing a hand against the wall, he kicked at the man until Nicholas stepped between them.

"Get out of my way," Matteo said, taking a step to the left to go around his cousin.

"He can't feel anything." Nicholas moved with him, blocking his way. "He's out cold."

It did not matter to Matteo. He did not want to stop until there was no more breath left in the other man.

Matteo faked right. Nicholas, however, knew him too well and continued to block him.

"Leave him." Nicholas pressed his hands against Matteo's chest and jerked his head in the direction of the apartment. "Go get Norma."

Matteo glanced over his shoulder at the little head peeping from behind the door, and his priorities immediately changed. She had already been through enough that afternoon and did not need to witness any more violence.

He returned to the apartment and knelt in front of the girl. "Are you all right?"

"I don't wanna search for clues anymore." Norma's voice was barely audible. "I wanna go home."

He gathered her in his arms and silently made the same promise he'd vowed to his daughter on the day she was born. No harm would ever come to her while he was around.

Holding her tight, he carried her out of the apartment. Nicholas stood in front of Lincoln's still body. One level down, Carmine stood over Lincoln's accomplice. Raymond stepped forward and held out his hands.

"I got her," Matteo announced, determined to deliver Norma back to Bailey himself.

Nicholas called from the fourth floor, "Let 'im go."

There was no pride in Raymond's gaze...only suspicion, doubt and anger. Yet he stepped to the side, allowing Matteo to pass.

Knowing how anxious Norma had to be to see her mother, and vice versa, Matteo sped down the side streets. Aside from an occasional sniffle, Norma sat silently by his side.

Matteo honked the horn when he turned the corner onto his uncle's block. Bailey, who had been sitting on her cousin's stoop with Celeste and Nonna, jumped up and ran to the curb. He shifted the car into park, and she yanked open the door. Tears ran down her cheeks when Norma scrambled out of the vehicle and into her arms.

"Are you okay?" Bailey asked, clinging to the girl.

"Yes, Mommy," Norma's reply was muffled by her mother's neck.

"Don't you ever go off with anyone again. Understand?"

Matteo suspected the command was unnecessary. The child had enough of a scare and would probably not leave her mother's side for a long time.

Still, Norma reassured her mother with another, "Yes."

Bailey stood up and glanced over her daughter's head. "Thank you."

"No need," he insisted. "Take care of her."

Bailey headed towards her cousin's place. She placed one foot on the step, then glanced back over her shoulder. "Lincoln?"

Matteo shook his head. He wished things could have turned out differently, but once her brother had kidnapped his niece, he'd sealed his fate.

Bailey's shoulders slumped. A tear rolled down her cheek. Without another word, she allowed Nonna to escort her inside.

Small arms wrapped around his waist. He looked down at his own daughter, who stared up at him with tears in her eyes.

"Thank you for helping my friend," Julia said.

"I'll always be there for both of you." His gaze moved to Eleanor.

The woman hesitated before the fight slowly faded from her. She nodded her head, raising his hopes of a future with his daughter.

"You should have someone take a look at your arm," Celeste said.

Matteo glanced at the swollen limb that had been throbbing ever since it was hit. He did not remember being in so much pain after his father broke his hand with a pipe for stealing from the family. But, at that time, he had been high and not remembering much of anything.

"You need a ride?"

He shook his head as he placed the keys in his cousin's hand. "I'll be fine," he insisted. "Take care of Bailey." He shuffled to the bus stop.

Chapter Twenty-Four

"What do you want?" Matteo grumbled as Nicholas climbed out of the blue sedan parked in front of his building. After a night sitting in the emergency room, he was not up to another warning to stay away from his family. All he wanted was to slip under the covers and sleep for the rest of the day.

"Come on." Nicholas's abrupt tone said refusing was not an option.

With a sigh, Matteo approached the car and slid into the passenger seat. He relaxed slightly at the empty back seat. If his cousin had been there to teach him another lesson, he would have brought help. Of course, there was always the possibility they were going to meet up with the accomplices someplace where there were fewer witnesses.

Matteo leaned his head back and closed his eyes. He was sore, tired, and did not have the energy to care anymore. He would deal with his fate when the time came.

The driver's door slammed shut and the car rolled away from the curb.

"What did the doctor have to say?" Nicholas asked.

"I've gotta wear the cast for six weeks," Matteo replied, wishing he could clock Lincoln one more time for his misery. He had only been wearing the cast for two hours and his arm was already hot and itchy, and the throbbing had yet to subside.

"Be glad you're right-handed."

"Just drive the fucking car," he grumbled.

Matteo was not in the mood for a Pollyanna outlook on things. He had not been fond of the overly positive girl and her "glad game" when his grandmother read the story to him and his cousins when he was six. Twenty years had not changed his opinion of the character.

Nicholas chuckled. Matteo did not appreciate his cousin finding amusement in his misery, but at least the other man shut up.

All too soon, Nicholas was shaking his shoulder, pulling him out of his blissful rest. Matteo grumbled as he shoved opened the car door. He stepped out and fell silent upon recognizing the cars lined up in front of brownstones on either side of the block.

It was a rarity for the Santiano family to gather anytime outside of birthdays, anniversaries, and holidays. Therefore, Matteo's suspicions rose, knowing his father, brothers, uncles and cousins were meeting at Marco Santiano's house first thing on a Sunday morning.

He suspected the outcome would be grave, but he had no more fight left in him. He was resigned to accept whatever verdict and punishment they were ready to dole out for his blatant disregard of the rules of his banishment.

Matteo dragged his feet up the steps to the parlor level. Boisterous but jovial chatter drifted from inside when Nicholas pushed open the front door. It sounded like a typical family gathering in which several conversations were going on at once. There were no talks of politics or business, and jokes were kept civil so nothing could be taken the wrong way and no feelings hurt.

All the conversations instantly ceased when Matteo stepped into the living room. Ten sets of eyes settled on him as he stood in the doorway, wary of the outcome of the meeting but too tired to run from his fate.

"Sit." Marco Santiano pointed to an empty dining room chair across from the green armchair that served as the man's throne.

When he was a child, Matteo was intimidated by his uncle. The man towered over everyone. When he spoke, people listened—and only the foolish questioned his decisions.

Standing before the man, Matteo felt like he was a seven-year-old boy being called to task for a misdeed.

Matteo's father and Uncle Joey sat on either side of the man. Their expressions were unreadable, but there was no doubt they would abide by whatever decree was announced.

Matteo dropped onto the seat, ready to meet his fate for disobeying the terms of his banishment. Not that he regretted or would change anything. He'd seen Bailey realize her dreams, he got one night with the woman of his heart, and he had been there to help her.

"Many times, I questioned your father's wisdom in sparing your life. But since it was the only favor he's ever asked of me, I agreed to honor his wishes," his uncle announced. "However, I've kept tabs on you, in the event you turn on that girl who also insisted on trusting you."

Matteo had been certain they had not known about his relationship, since no one had paid him a visit to tell him in the most painful way they could think of to leave Bailey alone.

"I didn't know what they saw in you, but yesterday

you did not betray their trust. Because of your actions, you are welcomed back into the family."

Matteo was speechless. His uncle's declaration opened a wealth of possibilities for him. He would never be denied the opportunity to be present during an emergency involving either of his parents. He could visit his daughter without the fear of Eleanor dragging her away. And he could be with Bailey…if she was willing to be with him.

While the events of the previous day got him back into the family, there was the likelihood it could also make him estranged from the woman he loved.

Bailey had lost her brother, the last link to her immediate family. And while it had been Lincoln's actions that had sealed his fate, she might still blame Matteo.

At the insistence of his family—a word he would never take for granted again—Matteo toasted his return with the men before they excused themselves so they could join their families for Sunday outings.

Despite his uncle's declaration, Matteo knew his past sins were not erased from everyone's mind. The glares from his brothers said it would take time before he regained their trust.

"I'll give you a ride," Nicholas said.

Before Matteo could accept the offer, he had one request, "May I see the twins?"

Nicholas nodded to the back door.

They cut across the yard, which had been extended with the removal of the stone wall, and entered the house next door. Upstairs, Matteo waited in the hall as Nicholas stepped into the bedroom. He strained to hear the whispered exchange, but all he could make out was a yawned, "Okay."

Nicholas returned to the door and waved him into the room. A mountain of packages was stacked in the corner by the window. There was only one crib, pushed against the wall. Matteo assumed a second bed would be added when the infants were a little older.

Georgia sat in a rocking chair, holding a baby in blue against her diaper-covered shoulder. Celeste paced the floor with the pink-clad infant in her arms.

"Come in," Georgia said.

"I'm not gonna stay long. I just wanted to see them."

"This one's Giorgio." The baby burped and she praised his accomplishment as only a proud mother could.

"And this quiet one is Nicolette," Celeste crooned.

Matteo wondered if a child born to Bailey and him would possess the same light brown complexion, curly hair, and hazel eyes as his cousin's babies.

Celeste held the sleeping baby out to him. Unwilling to try to hold her with only one good arm, he settled for kissing her forehead.

"*Sono bellissimi*," he said. "They're beautiful."

"Thank you," Georgia said.

Nicholas stepped to his wife's side as she pushed up from her chair. He hovered next to her, his arms outstretched, ready to catch her if she should stumble.

Georgia rolled her eyes, but she did not scold her husband for being extra vigilant. Instead, she kissed his cheek.

The exchange made Matteo long for a relationship of his own. More specifically, he wanted what his cousin had, but with Bailey.

"I'm ready," he announced.

Nicholas kissed his wife and children before escorting Matteo back outside. The cars that had been double-parked in front of the two houses were gone and peace had settled over the neighborhood until the next family gathering.

"What are your plans?" Nicholas asked after they climbed in the car.

Matteo shrugged. It wasn't that he did not know what he wanted to do. He just didn't want to share the dreams before he spoke to the woman he wanted to fulfill them with.

There was much to think about, including living arrangements, work, school, and—most importantly—whether she still wanted to be with him.

With his mind on the future and not where they were going, it took him a second to recognize his surroundings when the car stopped.

"Don't fuck it up this time," Nicholas advised him.

The well-meaning advice was unnecessary. If Matteo had learned anything, it was to cherish what he had.

He stepped out of the car and watched Bailey for clues to his next move. She sat on the steps with Norma and stared back at him, until he feared his dreams would not be realized.

****

In the eight years Bailey had known Matteo, she had seen a range of emotions—from exasperation to rage to contentment—decorate his features. After he had been declared dead to his family, there had been concern in his eyes when he took a chance and approached her in the diner. But what she had never seen previously was the doubt that flickered in his eyes as he stood by the car waiting for her to make the first move.

The man was not perfect, but then who was?

While Matteo had made mistakes, his good deeds outweighed the bad. Time and time again, he had gone out of his way to help her. While many would have turned their backs on a scared girl, he'd reassured her everything would be all right before taking her to the hospital. When others were ready to give up on her, he believed in her dreams and cheered her on. And, while he had failed to save her brother, he'd protected what was most precious to her.

Bailey patted Norma's shoulder. The girl raised her head from her mother's lap and looked in the direction she pointed. Her face lit up. She jumped up from the stoop, ran to him, and threw her arms around his waist.

Bailey glanced past Matteo to his cousin, who had climbed out of the car and leaned on the roof on the driver's side. Nicholas nodded, silently informing her that Matteo was once again accepted by his family.

Her gaze returned to Matteo. He held out his good arm. She stepped into his embrace and laid her head on his shoulder.

"Where do we go from here?" Bailey asked.

Matteo kissed her forehead and whispered, "Home."

A word about the author...

Ursula Renée crafts stories with diverse characters who must question their beliefs to find their happily-ever-after. She prefers the early to mid-twentieth century, when people began challenging society's conventions and expressing their individuality.

http://www.ursularenee.com

www.ingramcontent.com/pod-product-compliance
Lightning Source LLC
Chambersburg PA
CBHW052024020726
47501CB00004B/1234